Revenge

A Memphis Cold Case Novella

The sequel to
Justice Delayed

By Patricia Bradley

Text copyright © 2017 by Patricia Bradley
A Rights Reserved
Patricia's website: ptbradley.com

This book is a work of fiction. Names, characters, places, and incidents either are products of the author's imagination or are used fictitiously. Any resemblance to actual persons, living or dead, events, or locales is entirely coincidental.

To my family and to Bryan, for your support in this writing journey.
But most of all to Jesus, who gives me the words.

Acknowledgments

I couldn't have written this story without the help of my friend in the Cold Case Unit at the Memphis Police Department, Sargent Joe Stark

CHAPTER ONE

The full moon reflected on the Mississippi River as the cool wind sent shivers through Andi Hollister. She shook the fog from her brain and stared at the University of Memphis hoodie in her hands. Another chill raced over her. She slipped the hoodie on and turned, catching sight of a bronze monument. A man in a boat.

Maybe the chill came from not knowing why she sat on a bench at Tom Lee Park in downtown Memphis.

Not again.

No! It wasn't like before when she had a problem with pain pills.

She balled her hands, wincing at the sharp pain in her right hand. Opening her fingers, she eyed the cross on the key ring Will had given her. *Will.* He loved her. Didn't he? Yes. *But he'd been distant lately.* He wasn't happy about the pills, but she needed them for her back pain.

Andi brushed her thoughts away and concentrated on why she was here. Bit by bit, she recalled the interviews and then wrapping up the news segment for WLTZ on the homeless in the park. Nothing after that. How long ago had that been?

She checked her phone for the time. Eleven thirty-eight. Almost an hour and a half since she reported live on the ten o'clock news. The phone buzzed in her hand. A text from Treece. One of eleven.

Where are you!!? Why aren't you answering your phone? Will's been here, looking for you.

Revenge

Why was Will looking for her? They didn't have a date tonight after the broadcast. *Did they*? He was supposed to take his mother out to eat, and Andi was pretty sure he hadn't mentioned coming by the apartment after that. She checked the volume and texted back. *Phone's been on silent. On my way home.*

Immediately her cell buzzed with Treece's incoming call, and she slid her thumb across the bottom of the phone. "Hey," she said.

"Where have you been?" Her best friend's voice blasted her eardrum.

Andi held the phone away from her head. "I'm fine. You don't have to worry about me."

"Not worry about you? Your first day back at work since you hurt your back again, and you disappear for two hours?"

"My back is better, and it hasn't been that long since the broadcast. What did Will want?"

"He didn't say. Are you still taking pain pills?"

Andi did not want to deal with this right now. "Look, I'll be home in fifteen minutes. We'll talk then." Not only was Treece her best friend and co-worker at the TV station, but they had adjoining apartments in a converted house in Midtown, a fact she regretted at the moment.

"Okay, but be careful."

"Yes, ma'am." If anyone accosted her, she could always use the self-defense moves she'd learned. Andi's hand shook as she pocketed her phone and then rummaged through her purse for the Lortab bottle.

Her hand stilled. No. It hadn't been three hours, much less the six she was supposed to wait. She didn't have anything to take a pill with, anyway. She'd left her water bottle somewhere.

"Miss…"

She jumped and jerked her head toward the man's voice. One of the men she'd interviewed stood mere feet from her.

"I'm sorry, didn't mean to scare you."

"I didn't hear you come up." She pressed her hand to her thumping chest and looked past him, scanning the area. At the far end of the park a few people strolled near the riverbank. Her tension eased, barely.

"You don't need to be here alone," he said.

"Yes, you're right. I…I'm leaving right now."

"May I walk you to your car? It's not safe here."

But was she safe from him? When she interviewed him, he'd refused to reveal his name or the reason he was homeless. Since his clothes hadn't been tattered and dirty, she'd figured he was new to the streets.

"No. I'm fine by myself." She almost said she knew judo, but he would probably laugh. Not that she'd ever used it outside of class.

He shrugged then backed off. "Just trying to help."

She stood. "Thank you."

With a backward glance she struck out across the grass, ignoring the dew that soaked her shoes. The sooner she got to her car, the better. Moonlight blended with the overhead street lamps, casting ghostly shadows on the park, and goose bumps raised on her arms. Anyone could be hiding in those shadows.

Tension eased when she spotted her car in the parking lot. She'd done some dumb things in the past, but lingering at Tom Lee Park after the news report ended ranked at the top of the list. She couldn't recall why she wanted to stay after the cameraman encouraged her to leave with him.

Footsteps pounded the sidewalk behind her. Before Andi could react, a man grabbed her from behind, his muscled arm gripping her in a chokehold. It was too late to drop her chin like she'd been taught in the self-defense class, but still she struggled to break the hold. The odor of sweat tinged with musky cologne gagged her.

"Where's Chloe?" The man's guttural voice sent a chill down her back.

Why would he want to know the whereabouts of the teenaged

girl Andi had rescued from the streets? "I don't know."

"I don't believe you." He tightened his hold, cutting off her air. "Where is she hiding?"

She jerked her head back, butting him in the face and heard the satisfying crunch of cartilage breaking.

He loosened his hold. She stepped sideways, kicking at his groin. Missed. His arm tightened again. Andi bent over, yanking him over her shoulder.

He landed on the ground and scrambled up, blood streaming from his nose and his muscled chest heaving. She caught her breath. *Jason Boyd.* Explained a lot. Jason had been Chloe's pimp. A flash of silver sliced the air as he crouched with a knife in his hand, ready to spring.

Andi planted her feet.

"Leave her alone!"

The homeless man from earlier.

"No! Stay out of this," she yelled. "He has a knife!"

"You want a piece of this?" Jason turned on him.

"Come on, man. People are watching. Somebody's called the cops by now. You better beat it."

"Not before I teach you a lesson."

Before Andi could move, Jason plunged his knife into her would-be rescuer's chest. She screamed, and he wheeled on her. He took a step toward her and she palmed her hands up, close together. "You better leave before the cops come."

He hesitated. "Where is Chloe?"

"I told you, I don't know."

He rushed her, and she executed another move she'd practiced over and over in class, crisscrossing her hands with lightning speed against his wrist. The knife flew out of his hand, and she shoved her right hand toward his nose.

Jason ducked back and her hand hit air. With a curse, he slammed his left fist against her head. Her ears rang and pinpoint dots filled her vision. Andi went down to her knees. A frenzy of punches battered her head and body. Somewhere she heard a scream and realized it came from her own mouth.

Blocks away, sirens drew near, and the attack suddenly stopped. He bent near her ear. "You haven't seen the last of me."

Seconds later, his running footsteps faded away. Andi struggled to her feet. The homeless man who had come to her aid lay crumpled on the ground, blood spurting from the wound in his chest.

She had to stop the blood flow and peeled off her jacket and pressed it against his chest. If he died because of her, she would never forgive herself.

Revenge

CHAPTER TWO

Will Kincade pulled into the hospital lot on two wheels and parked in a spot reserved for police vehicles. He might be working cold cases instead of active homicides, but the parking sign didn't specify a certain unit. Will grabbed his jacket to cover the gun on his belt and hustled out of the car and through the ER doors.

Inside, he shrugged into the jacket as he approached the desk. "What room is Andi Hollister in?" he asked. Were they hiring high schoolers now? The teenage boy who couldn't seem to find Andi's name looked much too young to be a nurse.

"Exam room 6," he finally said.

"Thanks." Will turned and walked to the double doors.

"You can't go back there unless you're family!"

Will flashed his badge. "It's a police matter."

Besides that, he was practically family, and if Andi had come home right after her newscast, she would be wearing his ring instead of almost losing her life.

His fingers closed around the small velvet box in his pocket. He should've left it locked in the glove compartment. Because he wasn't proposing in the ER. And if what he suspected was true, he might not be proposing at all. At least not until Andi got help for her problem.

Someone had pulled back the curtain over the window in room six. Andi lay with her eyes closed in the dim light, her coppery hair fanning the pillow. His heart hitched at the purple bruise that covered her swollen right cheek. Blood had pooled beneath the skin under her eye. A real shiner. Tears glistened on her cheeks, and she swiped them away from the uninjured cheek with the back of her hand.

Will clenched his hands. He'd find the scum who did this to Andi, and he'd...he blew out a breath. He'd bring him to justice.

Andi sat up and her hair fell softly around her shoulders as she pulled a pill bottle from her purse. Lortabs, he was pretty sure.

"Hey," he said softly as he stepped into the room. "Should you be taking your own medicine?"

Andi stiffened. "My head is killing me, and I'm tired of waiting for the nurse to bring me something." She hesitated then dropped the bottle back into her purse and reached for a tissue. "Maybe I'll give her a couple more minutes."

He wished he'd been wrong, but the pills confirmed what he feared after she'd dropped her Narcotics Anonymous meetings. She was dependent on them again. He swallowed his disappointment and mustered a smile. "Probably a good idea. How are you feeling?"

"Like I've been flattened with a steam roller." She pressed the tissue against her eyes and then gave him a weak smile in return. "How did you—"

"Treece. When you didn't show up at home, she called your cell and didn't get an answer. A policeman called her back. It seems her call helped them locate your phone. Then she called me. I figure she'll be here any minute."

"I must be out of it—I hadn't even thought about my phone," she said. "Does my brother know?"

"I think Brad would be here if he knew." Her brother was a cold case detective like Will, and he was surprised one of the other policemen hadn't called him. "I told Treece I would take care of letting him know. Morning will be soon enough."

"Thanks. I don't think I could take one of his lectures right now."

"What *were* you doing in the park that late?"

Andi folded her arms across her chest and looked past him. "Did you see my nurse? I really need something for this headache."

Revenge

"When was the last time you had a pain pill?"

"Not now, Will." She held out a limp icepack. "If you want to be helpful, you could get this refilled."

She was right. This wasn't the time to discuss her drug addiction. He clamped his jaw shut and took the white bag.

After Will emptied the water, he found an aide who refilled the icepack. When he returned to Andi's room, she lay with her eyes closed. He gently placed the bag on her cheek.

Her brown eyes fluttered open. "Thanks," she whispered. "The man that tried to help me. Do you know if he's in this hospital or how he is?"

Will shook his head. "I'll ask at the desk."

The man wasn't a patient so Will called the detective who investigated Andi's attack and learned the other victim had been taken to the Med and that he was in surgery. When he returned to Andi's room, he relayed the information.

"He was trying to help me," she said, her voice cracking. "I hope he doesn't die."

"You're not to blame." The miserable look on her face said she thought otherwise. "I understand you recognized your attacker."

"I wouldn't have if he hadn't asked about Chloe. Then I remembered his mug shot." She shook her head, wincing. "I could've passed Jason Boyd on the street and never have known it."

"Exactly what did he say?"

She shuddered. "That I haven't seen the last of him. Why do you think he wants Chloe so badly?"

Will had no answer for that. Pimps usually didn't risk jail time to get one of their girls back. "Have you heard from her since she was put into hiding?"

"No."

A shadow crossed the door, and Will turned. Treece had arrived and the expression on her creamy brown face looked none too happy as she stormed into the room.

"Girl, what do you mean getting into this trouble!"

"Don't start," Andi said, palming her hands. The ice bag slipped from her face.

A small gasp escaped past Treece's lips. "Oh, that must hurt."

"It does." Andi placed the ice on her cheek again.

Treece bent over and gave Andi a gentle hug. "I'm so sorry, but what in the world were you doing at Tom Lee Park after the newscast?"

Andi's lips twitched. "Have you heard from Chloe lately?"

"What does she have to do—"

"My attacker was looking for her."

"Andi ID'd her attacker," Will said. "It was Chloe's pimp."

Treece's lips formed a small "o". "Jason Boyd. I hope he doesn't find out where she's in drug rehab."

Chloe was in rehab? Maybe he could use that as leverage to get Andi into the same place where she would at least be safe from Boyd. The problem would be convincing her.

Revenge

CHAPTER THREE

Jason sprinted across Riverside Drive, cursing as he took the steps to the top of the river bluff two at a time. He'd been following the reporter for days now, and he should've finished her off when he had the chance. She'd humiliated him and caused trouble with the higher ups. But he wanted her to suffer first. And then there was the matter of getting Chloe Morgan back. If he didn't recover her, he was a dead man walking.

Because of Chloe's blonde hair and blue eyes, the Russian wanted her for his Middle Eastern stable, and what the Russian wanted, he got. Or someone paid.

At the top of the steps, he hesitated. Take the Riverwalk back to his car or cut through the condos? The Riverwalk. He might encounter security in the condos. Jason pivoted left and jogged north on the walk.

The evening hadn't been a total waste. He'd attached a GPS tracker inside the rear bumper of Andi Hollister's car to make it easier to follow her. She had to know where Chloe was and now, he could track the reporter. It was just a matter of time before she was his. Then he would get the information out of her and finally finish her off.

Revenge would be so sweet.

CHAPTER FOUR

Where was that nurse with the pain medication for her head? She shifted her gaze from the door to Will, her heart skipping a beat. He'd come as soon as he'd learned she was in the ER. He was the best thing in her life, but now Will stared at her like he was waiting for an answer to something.

"What?" Andi said.

"Did you know Chloe was in rehab?"

"Rehab? No, but it makes sense. She was pretty strung out when we rescued her."

"We almost got her killed," Treece said. "I don't know how I let you talk me into going down on Beale Street with you. Should've stayed at the TV station where we belonged instead of trying to play cops."

Andi didn't like to think about that part of it. She hadn't been thinking clearly when she asked the fourteen-year-old girl to meet them. Her pimp had retaliated by trying to kill all three of them. Treece had been hurt along with Chloe and had been on sick leave from the TV station for almost a month. "How did you find out where she was?" she asked.

"Do you know where she is?" Will asked.

They'd both spoken at the same time. Treece sat on the side of the bed and answered Andi's question first. "The U. S. Marshal told Reggie yesterday, and he told me today."

Revenge

"So you two are on again?" Andi asked. Reggie Lane was Treece's fiancé, this month at least. It seemed she returned his engagement ring every other month.

"As long as he doesn't try to tell me what to do," her friend replied with a wry grin. Then Treece turned to Will. "She's at Living Free."

"The facility near Paris Landing?" Will asked.

Why did he sound so surprised? Andi had heard of the renowned drug rehabilitation facility located in a remote area of West Tennessee, mostly from her brother and Will after she admitted she *might* have a problem with painkillers. Since then she'd decided she didn't really have a problem. She didn't take that many Lortabs, only when her back pain flared up, and she had no desire to go to anything stronger. Why did everyone have to keep bugging her about it?

"You two said you wanted to get more of Chloe's story for the second part of your human trafficking documentary…" Will let his voice trail off.

"He's right," Treece said. "You could get in there and interview her."

"Yeah," Will said. "It would be the perfect opportunity, and it'd get you away from Jason Boyd until we catch him."

"There's a small problem." Andi narrowed her eyes at them. "To get into Living Free, you need to have a drug addiction problem, and I don't."

"Are you sure about that?" Treece said. "Seems to me, you've been taking a lot of those Lortabs."

"I agree," Will said.

Andi folded her arms across her chest and winced. Even the slightest movement made her hurt in places she hadn't thought existed. "I do not have a problem. Not anymore, anyway," she said through gritted teeth. What was this? An intervention?

Will caught her gaze and held it. "Then explain why you stayed behind at Tom Lee Park after the film crew left."

Andi lay back on the pillow and pulled the white sheet to her neck before she placed the ice bag on her cheek. "I...I don't want to talk about it right now."

Treece squeezed her arm. "We're not saying you have a major problem with drugs, but it would be an opportunity to talk to a different set of counselors. Not to mention you'd get to see Chloe again. And it'd be a great opportunity to do research for the documentary you talked about on drug rehab."

Andi released her death grip on the sheet. When she first started going to NA, she *had* talked about doing a documentary. She turned her head toward the door, and relief spread through her body as her nurse entered.

"I finally got something for your headache. Sorry it took so long." The nurse poured water in a glass and handed her the pills in a small cup.

"Thank you." She peered into the cup. "What is it?"

"Tylenol."

That wasn't strong enough. She caught the words before they flew out of her mouth, but she couldn't believe she'd waited all this time for Tylenol. "Thanks."

She downed the tablets. As soon as Will and Treece left, she'd take two of her Lortabs.

"So if I decided to do the documentary, how would I get into Living Free? I'm sure there's a waiting list," she said when the nurse left.

Treece glanced at Will and he cleared his throat. "Um, the director went to school with Brad and me."

Andi stared at him. "And just like that, he'll take me. No notice?"

"It's a she. Brad talked to her earlier this week." Will froze. A red flush spread up his neck to the tips of his ears.

"Brad talked to the director of Living Free about me?" Andi's voice sounded small in the dead quiet of the room.

"It wasn't like that." The words came out in a rush.

She couldn't believe Brad had gone behind her back. A thought stabbed her heart. "Whose idea was it to call her?"

He didn't have to answer. His red face did it for him. "Yours? How could you without talking to me first?"

Will's jaw shot forward. "I wanted some options for you when we talked."

"Hey guys," Treece said. "I'm going to get a cup coffee."

Andi nodded, her gaze never leaving Will's blue eyes. "When did you plan to have this talk?"

Will pulled a chair next to the bed and sat down. "Tonight. I'm worried about you."

"Don't be. I'm fine."

"No, you're not. You shouldn't still be taking those pain pills."

"You'd take them if you were in pain," she retorted. He had no idea how much her head hurt right now.

"How bad was the pain when you took one at the park? Or did you take two?"

"It was bad enough." Her cheeks heated under his steady gaze, and she looked away, unable to bear seeing the disappointment in Will's eyes. Her back hadn't actually been hurting, and she'd wanted to keep it that way. Besides, she'd needed the boost the pills gave her to get through the TV segment. Okay, maybe not two, but when both of them tumbled out of the bottle, she'd popped them into her mouth without thinking.

"I saw the look on your face when the nurse brought Tylenol instead of something stronger," he said. "And how about now? When I leave, are you going to take one of those pills in your purse? Or maybe two?"

She ignored his question, and he paced the room, refusing to look at her. "Come on, Will. You know I can stop taking the pills anytime I decide."

He stopped. "Don't you think it's time you decided to do that?"

She gaped at him. His voice held an or-else tone. The throbbing in her head reached a crescendo. She did not need this right now. "Is that an ultimatum?"

His shoulders slumped and he pressed his lips together. Then he nodded. "I guess it is."

A vise-like band squeezed her chest. She got it that his mother had abandoned him as a child because of her addictions, but she wasn't abandoning him. Andi gritted her teeth. She was not a drug addict.

"And I guess I have my answer," he said. He sucked in a deep breath. "As much as I love you, I can't handle this." He palmed his hand toward the bed. "I'm sorry."

Without another word, he turned and walked out the door.

"Fine. Be that way." If he heard her, he didn't bother to acknowledge her words. She leaned against the pillow and closed her eyes. She couldn't bear to see the emptiness of the room. But she better get used to it. If Will could walk out on her that easily, maybe they didn't belong together.

CHAPTER FIVE

Had Treece left her as well? Andi smoothed a wrinkle on the hospital bed. How would she get home, now that Will left? Worse came to worse, she'd call a cab. Relief flooded her when her friend stuck her head inside the door.

"Will gone?"

"Yeah."

"You've been crying."

"No, I haven't." At least not much.

Treece lifted her eyebrows and gave her "the look" that said *I don't believe you.* "What happened?"

"He's upset that I won't go to rehab." That was all she needed to know.

"He wants what's best for you." Treece hesitated, and then added gently, "And so do I."

"Come on, you know I don't need to go to rehab."

"Do I? Yeah, there for a few months you did really well, but this past month—"

"I had back spasms."

"That's just it. You take the pain pills instead of therapy. Or even finding out if surgery will help. Maybe two weeks at Living Free is what you need—to understand why you take pills."

How many times did Andi have to say it? "I wouldn't take them if I didn't have pain."

"Really? Were you having back spasms tonight?"

"No, but—"

"No buts. You have a problem, Andi, and you need to deal

with it."

A lead weight settled in her stomach as she remembered coming to and realizing she was alone at the park with no idea of how she'd gotten there. It had scared her almost as much as the time she'd run the red light in the middle of the night and almost creamed a pickup. What if everyone was right?

"It'd be good research for the documentary…and like Will said, it'd get you away from Jason Boyd."

The ache in her heart doubled down. Maybe if she went, Will would change his mind about their relationship. No. The damage was done. She didn't know that she could forgive him for walking out on her. Even if she did still love him, his demand that she get treatment was unreasonable.

But what if she lost him for good? She couldn't imagine life without him, but she might have to. And that made her mad all over again.

Treece sat on the edge of the bed. "Since it will be work related, I bet you won't even have to use up all your personal time."

Andi weighed her options. Maybe it wouldn't hurt to talk to different counselors. Treece said two weeks. Andi could do anything for fourteen days, even though she didn't *really* have a problem. If she were listing pros and cons, the cons would have a longer list that included doing research for their documentary.

"If I went to Living Free, I can leave anytime?"

Treece took her hand and squeezed it. "Sure, but you want to stay for at least two weeks."

Andi squared her shoulders. "Okay, but could you and Brad take me? We can drive my car up and you can ride back with him."

"You don't want Will to take you?"

"No." At this moment she wasn't sure she ever wanted to see him again.

***

Will opened his car door then paused to stare up at the fourth floor. He'd hung around the nurses' station until Andi was admitted for the night. For observation, he'd heard the ER doctor tell the charge nurse.

Go to her. Apologize for leaving. Will steeled his heart against his desire. It wasn't that he didn't want to, but if he did, it would give Andi false hope. It didn't matter how much he loved her, he couldn't be with her as long as she denied she had a drug problem.

It wasn't the drug addiction that drove him away. It was her denial of it. It was his mother all over again, only her drug of choice had been alcohol. Cass would blow into town, broke and down on her luck after her latest boyfriend kicked her out. And his Aunt May, who raised Will, always let her crash with them.

His aunt had thought it would bring Will and his mother together, and for a few days after she dried out, Cass would try to bond with him. Will begged her to not drink, but she would lie and tell him what he wanted to hear. At night he'd hear his aunt and mother argue, his mom insisting she didn't have a problem.

Then she'd get restless, and soon would come the nights when she'd dress up and spritz herself with cheap perfume and go out. On the mornings she bothered to come home, she smelled like cigarette smoke and whiskey. Before long, Cass would be gone again, and they wouldn't hear from her for months.

Will shook the thoughts off and got into his car. He couldn't bear the disappointment again.

CHAPTER SIX

Andi shivered as she entered the activity room at Living Free. Someone had forgotten to bump up the air conditioner yesterday, and she pulled the University of Memphis hoodie tighter. In the past week she'd changed her mind three times about entering the rehab facility, but in the end she'd come, mostly to get everyone off her case.

And after listening to the other women in her group talk about their addictions, Andi was convinced more than ever she didn't belong here. The others had used drugs she'd never thought of trying. Heroin. Meth. Cocaine. The one bright spot had been connecting with Chloe.

Her mind wandered to Will. She'd hoped when he discovered she was going into rehab, he would offer to give her a ride. But his silence told her all she needed to know—their relationship was over. She was beginning to wonder if he'd ever loved her.

Andi brushed the thoughts off and glanced around the room. It was a calm place with dusty blue walls and chairs arranged in a half circle on the lighter blue carpet. She wasn't the first one here because in the corner, a silver coffee service with thick, restaurant-style mugs beckoned. She answered its call. At least coffee would knock off the chill, and sipping it would make a nice distraction if she needed it later. A painting of a tree bending with the wind, its leaves blowing freely away captured Andi's attention, just as it had each time she came to the twice a day group sessions. Probably intended as a metaphor for breaking free of addictions.

A cultured voice called her name and she turned. Doctor

Lillian Sullivan. Andi had met the petite psychologist her first day at Living Free and liked her so far. But then she hadn't dug too deeply into Andi's psyche.

"Sit wherever you'd like," Doctor Sullivan said, the invitation rolling pleasantly off her tongue.

Andi took a couple of sips from the mug, and then took a seat at the end. If today followed the other days, every other seat would be filled first. But a woman about her size took the chair next to Andi, surprising her. Roxie, if she remembered correctly, and Roxie never spoke unless she had to, and rarely made eye contact. Right now, she looked like a waif with her long dark hair and big brown eyes. Roxie ran her hands up and down her thin arms as she hugged them to her body.

"Where's your sweater?" Andi asked.

"Forgot it."

"Here, put this on." The coffee had warmed her, and after she fished the cross key ring from the pocket, she slipped out of the hoodie and handed it to her. The talisman gave her comfort when the sessions touched a nerve.

"Thanks. I don't know why it's so cold in here," Roxie said.

"Probably because someone forgot to bump the thermostat up when it cooled off last night."

Andi's attention shifted as a teenager entered the room with several other women. The teen grabbed a chair and pulled it over to the other side of Andi. Chloe Morgan. No, she corrected herself. Mackenzie Knight was the new name the witness protection people had given her. Not only a new name, but a new look as well. Her amber eyes were clear, unlike when she and Treece rescued the girl.

Andi liked the oversized jersey and jeans she wore today rather than the body hugging clothes the teenager had worn on the streets. She'd decided to let the platinum color grow out instead of coloring her hair again, and her long, straight hair had been cut short in a boyish bob. The girl-next-door look was a good fit for her.

Andi's heart broke for the teenager. Chloe had a hard life,

first her mother dying, then her stepfather's abuse. Andi didn't want to think about what she had gone through at the hands of that man. Then Jason Boyd had promised to protect her, but he turned out even worse than the stepfather when he sold her on the streets. But now things were looking up, and Chloe was getting counseling for what she'd endured in her young life. A second chance, she called it.

"How are you doing?" Andi asked.

"I don't want to leave," she replied, eyeing Andi's face.

The concealer did a fair job of covering the fading bruises if no one looked too closely like Chloe was doing now. So far she hadn't told her what had happened, and she hoped the girl wouldn't ask questions in front of everyone. "How do you feel about a run later this afternoon? We can talk then."

Chloe nodded as her gaze slid past Andi to Roxie. "Sure."

They both turned toward the front as Dr. Sullivan sat in a chair facing the circle.

"It looks like a few people will be late this morning, but I'd like to go ahead and get started. Anyone want to be first to tell us how it's going today?" For a second, no one moved, and then the hand of one of the other women went up. "Yes, Leslie?"

"Yesterday when Andi was talking, it sounded like she didn't think she had a problem with drugs." Leslie turned to face Andi. "I believe that's something we have to acknowledge before we can move forward."

Andi gripped the cross. She'd heard the brunette's story the first day. This was Leslie's third trip to rehab, so evidently she hadn't acknowledged her problem. Besides, they'd asked for honesty. Andi didn't need help for a problem she didn't have—she could quit taking the pain pills anytime she wanted to — as long as she had no pain.

"Maybe she's not there yet," Chloe said, then shot Andi an apologetic smile.

Et, tu, Brute? "I only took the pills when I was in pain so I could do my job, and they were prescribed pills at that."

"And you never took more than you were supposed to?" Leslie said.

"Not often."

"Are you lying to us or yourself? When was the last time you were actually in pain?"

Andi stiffened. When was the last time she'd had the debilitating pain that shot out of her back and down her leg? It'd been the reason she'd taken a few days off a month ago, but after a week of rest and Lortabs, the pain had gone away. What was so wrong about taking the pain pills to make sure it stayed away?

Suddenly, Leslie's face softened. "We're only trying to help you."

"I don't need your help. *If* I have a problem, I'll take care of it myself." Andi rubbed her thumb along the hard edges of the cross and tried not to think about the Lortab in her pocket. She'd stashed a few of the pills in the lining of her suitcase, just in case her pain flared up again. If everyone would stop harping every time she took the pills, she wouldn't have to hide them.

"So you never depend on anyone else?" Wonder tinged Roxie's voice.

"No." Andi cringed at how arrogant that sounded. "I mean, hardly ever."

"Maybe that's why you don't see you have a problem with pain killers," Leslie said.

They all sounded like Will, and Andi was tired of this. *Say whatever.* "Okay, maybe I have a *small* problem."

"You didn't say that like you meant it," Chloe said. "And there's no such thing as small problems with drugs. When I first came here, my excuse was the drugs were forced on me. It took me a while to admit I liked the way they made me feel."

Chloe might look like a teenager now, but she didn't always talk like one. Andi hated that life had given her an adult perspective.

"I know how she feels." Roxie's voice sounded small in the room. "And maybe she doesn't have as bad a problem as the rest of us. I don't know about the rest of you, but I like the way drugs make me feel and would take something right now if I could get my hands on it."

Silence fell into the room. Andi wanted to say she didn't like the way the Lortabs made her feel…but was it the truth? Would she take one now if she could? She rubbed the cross again. There was no denying the burst of energy the yellow tablets gave her, something she really needed in her job as a TV reporter. And if she was honest with herself there was no denying the desire sometimes, even though she didn't have pain. But she wasn't ready to admit that out loud yet.

"We all would," Leslie said. "Except I don't want to mess up again. I have too much to lose. That's why I'm here."

Had she already lost what she cared about most? Somewhere deep inside, Andi felt she hadn't lost Will. The desire to do whatever it took to get him back stirred in her heart. She took a deep breath. Maybe it was time to see why she craved the yellow pills.

Doctor Sullivan, who had been quiet, cleared her throat. "So what are you doing to redirect your thoughts?"

A couple of the women chimed in, describing how the Bible study at night had helped, and Andi loosened her grip on the cross, glad the attention had been diverted away from her. She kept quiet the rest of the session, her thoughts returning to how the Lortabs made her feel. She hadn't had one since arriving at rehab, but she'd thought about taking one often enough. It was like the more she tried not to think about them, the more she did. Another thing she wasn't going to admit out loud.

Chloe nudged Andi and she looked up. *The session was over?* She'd lost track of time.

"When do you want to meet?" the teenager asked.

"How about around twelve-thirty? That'll give us an hour before we have to be back here for another group session." Andi's insides curled at the thought of another session. Maybe she could plead a headache and stay in her room. She looked around for Roxie to get her hoodie, but the woman was gone.

Revenge

***

Jason lowered his binoculars, not believing his luck. After almost two weeks of not catching Andi Hollister by herself, here she was standing alone on the pier. Her back was to him, but it had to be her in that University of Memphis hoodie. He'd seen her yesterday with a group of women and she'd been wearing it. What were the odds of there being two women at the place with the same hoodie?

This might be his only chance to snatch her. And once he had her at the vacant cabin he'd found, he'd worm Chloe's location out of her one way or another. But he had to hurry before someone came up.

Taking care to not make any noise, he crept from the edge of the woods to the wooden pier, and then made a dash to where she stood. Before she could turn around, he slipped his arm around her neck, squeezing her windpipe in the crook of his arm. Unlike Monday night, this time he was quick enough in cutting off her air, and she slumped against him. He laid her facedown on the pier. Now to get her bound and to the all-terrain vehicle hidden a hundred yards from the lake before she came to.

He turned her over and groaned. This wasn't Andi Hollister.

CHAPTER SEVEN

At the far end of the lake, Andi bent over and placed her hands on her knees to catch her breath. She checked her watch. They'd only been on the trail bordering the lake for fifteen minutes? It seemed like an hour. Once her breathing returned to normal, she straightened, smelling the autumn scent of fallen leaves.

Dust motes from weeks of dry weather tinted the shafts of sunlight. With her allergies, jogging may not have been a good idea. Andi had been tempted to take a Lortab before they came out to the lake in case exercising aggravated her back. She hated to admit lack of opportunity was the only reason she hadn't. Surprisingly, her back wasn't hurting.

"Wait up," she called when Chloe kept her faster pace.

The teenager circled and jogged back, her brown hair bouncing. "You're out of shape."

"You're telling me? Walking okay?"

"Sure."

The girl fell in beside Andi, and the dry grass on the path crackled under their feet as they made their way back to the pier. "I've been meaning to tell you how well you look."

Chloe beamed at her. "Yeah. I feel better, too. You want to walk out on the pier for a few minutes before we have to go back?"

"Sure." When Chloe bounded on the pier, she didn't even try to keep up with the teenager, and she was already sitting at the end, her legs dangling over the water when Andi got there.

A cold front had blown through by noon, and it had turned into one of those November days when the sky was so blue it made

Revenge

Andi's heart swell to look up at it. It was hard to believe it was calling for storms by nightfall. At least everyone hoped it would rain with everything so dry. The sharp scent of pine drew her attention to the forest beyond the lake, casting a pall over her mood. Dark and forbidding, and from what she understood, the forest went on for over five thousand acres. Getting lost in it was not an option.

She'd been told that Living Free's designer had intentionally set the rehab twenty-five miles from the nearest town to make the patients think twice about running. Not that they were prisoners, but there were rules to follow, and addicts were notorious for not following rules. If someone decided they wanted to leave, it was a long walk to town.

The distance to town was not lost on Andi either. She turned and scanned the parking lot, finding her Corolla near the building where Treece had parked it. It was one of the conditions she'd laid down before she came to Living Free. Knowing it was here gave her peace, even though she'd have to ask the administrator for the keys if she wanted to leave.

Andi still found herself slipping her hand in her pocket for her cell phone, only to remember no patient was allowed to have one for the first month. She definitely chafed under some of the rules. But at least she had her computer even if she didn't have Internet and could work on her projects. And she'd taken to carrying the cross Will had given her in whatever pocket she had as a reminder of what might be waiting when she got out of rehab.

Beside her Chloe tossed a twig into the water, creating a circle of ripples.

Andi focused on the widening circle. The skin on the back of her neck prickled, and she glanced toward the forest again, seeing nothing but trees and undergrowth. Still, she couldn't shake the feeling someone watched them. She shook it off and turned to Chloe. "You said earlier you didn't want to leave. Why not?"

"I don't know where I'm going from here." She gave Andi a wry smile. "They can't put me in foster care—I might get someone killed."

It had to be hard, being in the witness protection program. Treece had told her Chloe was in a nine-month program here. "Are you that close to finishing?"

"Next month."

"Do you have any family?" She'd never heard Chloe talk about anyone except her stepfather.

"No. My grandparents came from the old country, and they only had one daughter—my mom, so I don't have any aunts or uncles, and my grandparents died years ago."

"Old country?"

"Latvia."

Andi had no idea what it would be like without having family around. She squeezed Chloe's arm. "Something is bound to open up before it's time to leave."

She felt responsible for the girl after she and Treece rescued her from Jason Boyd, a rescue that almost cost Chloe her life when someone fired at them from a black SUV. Chloe had always insisted it wasn't Jason who shot her, but Andi wasn't so sure.

"Who beat you up and gave you a black eye?" Chloe asked.

Andi touched her cheek, surprised she hadn't asked the question before they jogged. "How do you know I didn't have an accident?" she asked, turning to look at the girl.

Chloe cocked her head to the side and gave Andi the you-don't-think-I'd-buy-that look she remembered using as a teenager.

"That—" She pointed to her cheek. "Wasn't caused by any accident."

"Can't put anything over on you," Andi said with a grunt. She waffled about telling her, not sure how the girl would receive the news Jason was looking for her. "Someone attacked me."

"Why? Where were you?"

"Alone at Tom Lee Park after eleven at night." When Chloe shot her a puzzled look, Andi said, "It's in downtown Memphis— by the river."

Revenge

Chloe snorted. "Even I know better than to do something that stupid. What were you thinking?"

Andi crossed her arms. "It was a dumb thing to do, okay?"

"Did they catch the guy?"

Andi shook her head. "He got away, and they haven't found him yet."

"So you knew him?"

"Yep." Andi felt Chloe's gaze and turned to face her, almost able to see the wheels turning in her mind.

"It was Jason, wasn't it?"

Even though she knew Chloe was smart, her guess took Andi by surprise. "Yes."

The teen fisted her hands. "He's looking for me, isn't he?"

Again Andi answered with a simple yes, and Chloe buried her face in her hands. Andi scooted closer, putting her arm around her shoulders. "Why would he risk going to jail to find you?"

For a minute Chloe didn't answer, then she raised her head and looked out over the lake. Andi followed her gaze. Did Chloe sense they were being watched as well? "Do you see something?"

The girl shook her head. "Just trying to get my thoughts together. You see, I wasn't supposed to be on the streets that night. The higher ups had told Jason to get me ready to leave. But he was greedy, didn't think they'd find out."

"What do you mean, get you ready?" Andi wasn't sure she wanted to know.

Chloe dropped her gaze to the water. "A couple of nights before I met you…" she picked at the cuticle on her thumb. "There was this man. He wasn't from here. Jason called him the Russian. Black hair, black eyes…" she squeezed her eyes closed.

Andi touched her arm, and she flinched. "The counseling. Is it helping you to cope with what you've been through?"

"I don't know if there's enough help for that." The teenager swallowed. "I overheard Jason talking to somebody, and they were talking about me. Jason's boss had sold me to the Russian."

Chloe's voice dropped and Andi had to strain to catch the words. She couldn't imagine how that had made the girl feel. Andi smoothed back a strand of the girl's brown hair away from her face. "It's over," she said softly.

"It'll never be over," Chloe said. "Jason will find me and hand me over to them. He's a dead man if he doesn't."

Revenge

CHAPTER EIGHT

Two hours later, Jason returned to the lake to check on whether the body had been found. He took his binoculars from the backpack and braced against the fork of an oak tree. The woman hadn't been discovered, but it wouldn't be long. Two women had jogged past it and now were returning to the pier.

In the adrenaline rush, he hadn't realized the woman wasn't Hollister until he turned her over. He hadn't known she was even dead until he'd leaned closer to her and discovered she wasn't breathing. Then he'd felt for a pulse. Nothing. But how? Unless her heart had quit when he squeezed against her windpipe. She was in a drug rehab—probably had a bad heart after using.

Jason shook the memory away and focused on the two as they sat at the edge, their feet dangling over the water. He lowered the glasses. The one on the right was definitely Hollister this time. But who was the kid on the left?

He zoomed in on her face, and wished he had his camera with him. Jason had a facial recognition app on his computer and if she was on any of the social media sites, he could identify her. Probably just some kid the reporter had connected with at the rehab, but he would bring the camera when he returned. At any rate he couldn't nab Hollister now, not with another witness present. But the reporter wasn't going anywhere.

Andi Hollister in rehab. That had been a surprise. A text

buzzed into his phone and he checked it. The Russian's henchman, Razor. How he missed dealing with JD. But he was in prison now, and the Russian had taken his place in the organization. Or maybe he'd even bumped the top man that Jason had never met. Wolf, everyone called him. They all used aliases. JD, the Russian, Wolf, Razor. A text dinged on his phone. Razor. *Think of the devil...*

Do you have the reporter?

Not yet. He texted back.

Have you located her?

He hesitated. Lie or text Razor where she was? One of his own bodyguards texted him this morning the Russian had gotten tired of waiting for Jason to deliver and put a contract out on the streets for Andi Hollister's capture. Loyalty was not in his vocabulary, and if someone other than Jason brought Hollister or Chloe to the Russian, Jason was a dead man. No. He would let them know once he had Chloe's location and could deliver her. *Still working on it.*

He had to work fast, though.

Revenge

CHAPTER NINE

Andi wanted to tell Chloe that Jason Boyd would never find her, but life had taught the girl that might not be true. She was well acquainted with the power evil wielded. Andi rubbed Chloe's shoulder. "The U. S. Marshals are doing all they can to keep that from happening. And your friends—we're doing what we can, too."

"I know. Most of the time I don't worry about it. Not since learning about Jesus. I'm trying to let him do the battle for me, but it's not always easy." Chloe turned and glanced at the shore behind them.

Dullness in Andi's chest spread to her stomach. For years she had struggled with trusting God to bring good out of everything and here a fifteen year-old girl was way ahead of her.

Suddenly the teenager stiffened.

"What's wrong?"

"Is that someone floating in the water?" Chloe pointed to the left, toward the reeds growing out into the lake, then she gasped. "Isn't that the sweater you had on earlier?"

Andi searched the shoreline and found what Chloe was pointing to about a hundred feet from them. Andi's mouth went dry when she recognized the big M with a leaping tiger. She hadn't seen anyone with another one at the facility, so it had to be the hoodie she'd loaned Roxie. Which way to get to her? Swim or from the shore. Chloe answered for her by jumping into the water, and Andi followed.

The cold water took her breath, and it was deeper than she thought. She shook the chill off and struck out toward Roxie, beating

Chloe by a couple of strokes.

Andi found her footing in the shallower water. "Help me turn her over."

Roxie's dark lashes stood out against her gray face. Andi didn't need a doctor to tell her the woman was dead. "Let's get her to shore."

For such a thin woman, it was hard getting her to the bank with her waterlogged clothes.

"Do you think she killed herself?" Chloe asked once they had her body out of the water.

"I don't know." She hadn't thought the woman was suicidal. The sense of being watched flashed in Andi's mind and she jerked her head up to scan the nearby forest. Then a shout from the pier drew her attention. Leslie from the group rehab.

She waved at them. "Doctor Sullivan is looking for you!"

"Tell her to get help," Andi said.

***

Clouds had rolled in again by dinner time, and the distant rumbling of thunder hinted rain might be on its way as Andi got ready for bed. Or not. Someone said at dinner they would probably only get the thunder and lightning with a few drops of rain.

She hadn't been able to get Roxie's gray face out of her head. Doctor Sullivan had called them all together before dinner for an update. At this point, the assumption was Roxie fell while on the pier and drowned. Tragic, but there was nothing to indicate she'd taken her life. An autopsy would reveal more. Maybe.

Andi walked to her window that faced the lake and pulled the curtain back just as another bolt of lightning lit up the night sky. Seconds later thunder sent chills down her arms. Her third night here, and she missed Will so much it hurt. She wanted to believe he would be waiting for her when she returned home. That he would realize breaking it off was a big mistake.

Probably wouldn't happen, though. She was too much trouble. Not worth the effort.

Revenge

What if she acknowledged she had a problem with pain pills? Maybe then he'd change his mind. Her shoulder slumped. Who was she kidding? She opened the suitcase and unzipped the compartment where she'd stored the Lortabs. How could Andi convince him when she really didn't believe there was a problem? She could quit taking the pills anytime she wanted to. That she hadn't taken one of the pills she'd brought was proof.

Then throw them away.

Her hand shook. She could flush them down the toilet. But what if her back started hurting again? Andi put them back in the suitcase and walked back to the window. Lightning streaked from the clouds to the ground, illuminating a man standing on the pier. She froze. Then the darkness swallowed him.

When the next bolt streaked across the clouds, the pier was empty. She rubbed her eyes. She'd seen someone, she was certain of it. But how did they disappear so quickly? She waited for more lightning and when it came, there was no one there.

Could it be that talk about Jason this afternoon made her imagine seeing someone? Tomorrow she'd ask if anyone else had seen the man.

CHAPTER TEN

Will pulled his thoughts from Andi and re-read the cold case file in his hands, a murder from ten years ago. After the second paragraph, he closed the folder and laid it on his desk. Then he dialed Brad Hollister's number.

"Have you heard anything from your sister?"

"Not today. I talked with the director yesterday, and she indicated Andi had settled in," Brad said.

"I hope she finally admits she has a problem." Will still didn't know where their relationship would go from here. She might never forgive him for what happened at the hospital.

"Andi was really disappointed you didn't come with us."

Will's hand tightened on the phone. Brad's tone indicated he was disappointed as well. "I'm glad she's there, but I couldn't go with you to take her."

"But she was doing what you wanted her to do."

"That's just the point. She can't do this for me. Andi has to be there because she recognizes she has a problem and wants to fix it," Will said. "If she does it for any other reason, she'll be right back where she was sooner or later. Probably sooner." He looked up as Lieutenant Reggie Lane appeared at his doorway.

"Got a minute?"

"Brad let me get back to you." Will ended the call. "What's up?"

Revenge

"Last night vice busted a prostitute. I think you might want to talk to her. She's in Jason Boyd's stable of girls."

His pulse quickened. Like a ghost, Jason Boyd had disappeared after the attack on Andi. "Have you found him yet?"

Reggie shook his head. "She claims she hasn't seen him in a few days, that his second in command is running things. She's in the interrogation room on the seventh floor."

Will stood and followed Reggie to the elevator and then down to vice. He stopped in front of the two-way mirror to study the girl. A tattoo on the back of her neck. Probably Jason's brand. Couldn't be over eighteen. But she had the hard look of the streets, reminding Will of Chloe when he first saw her. He understood from Treece that Chloe hadn't even looked like the same girl when she saw her at Living Free.

"Name's Charity Hawkins, but goes by Rose on the streets," Reggie said, looking down at his clipboard.

The girl in the room glanced toward the mirror, hooking a strand of hair behind her ear. Then she winked even though she couldn't see him. A hard case. Probably wouldn't get anything out of her. He slipped inside the room and leaned against the wall with his arms folded.

She gave him a cursory glance then took a sip of the soda someone had brought her.

"Like I said before," Charity said, "I don't know where Jason Boyd is."

Reggie slid in a chair at the table as the detective who had been interrogating her stood. "She's all yours," he said and handed Reggie a folder before he walked out the door.

Reggie read over the paperwork as the girl ran her thumb up and down the soda can. "This is your third arrest this year so you're looking at eleven months and twenty-nine days."

She flinched and then gave him a sour look. "And what does the John get? Nothing. Hardly seems fair."

"We could work something out if you helped us find Boyd,"

Reggie said.

"Believe me, if I knew where he was, I'd tell you." She took a long sip of the drink.

"When did you see him last?"

"Been a few days. He came to the house and stuffed some clothes in a bag. Didn't tell anybody where he was going or when he'd be back."

"How about before that?" Will asked. "Did you overhear anything that might give a clue to where he's gone?"

She started to shrug and stopped, her eyes widening before she quickly dropped her gaze.

"You remembered something," Will said and walked closer to the table.

"Maybe." Charity tilted her head. "What will it get me?"

"Depends on whether it helps us find Boyd," Reggie said.

When Charity didn't answer, Will thought they'd lost her, and then the girl took a deep breath.

"A week before Jason took off, I didn't work, had a virus and he was afraid if I gave it to one of the Johns, they'd retaliate. Anyway, I was cleaning the bathroom downstairs that's right off the room he uses for an office. He was talking to someone and the other guy tells Jason he has to find that reporter Andi Hollister, that she would know where Chloe was."

"Who was the other guy?" Reggie asked.

"I don't know. Never heard his voice before. He spoke with some kind of accent—could've been Russian...I've heard this Russian cartel has taken over the trafficking business in Memphis." She rubbed her hands together. "Chloe was my friend and I hope they never find her, but..."

"But what?" Will demanded.

"Jason told the guy he would put a tracker on the reporter's car."

Will startled. "A tracker?" Was it possible Boyd had tracked Andi to the rehab? "Do you know if he did?"

Revenge

"I got a feeling he did. I heard him call somebody when he was packing. Told 'em he'd have the reporter by the end of the week." She raised her eyebrows. "I don't think they liked his answer."

"Why?" Reggie leaned forward.

"'Cause a couple of nights ago this guy calling himself Razor came around looking for him."

"Razor?"

"He works for the Russian guy, at least that's what one of the other girls said.

Will pushed his chair back. "I have to make a call."

He dialed Brad's number as he hurried out the door. "Boyd knows where Andi is," he said when his friend answered. "You need to call the rehab director and alert her."

"How did he find her?"

Will explained what Charity had told them. "Can you get away? I'm driving to the rehab."

"You bet. I'm out in East Memphis, so I'll meet you at my house."

Thirty minutes later Will picked up Brad. "Did you call the director?"

"She wasn't in, but I left word for her to call me back. And for her to allow Andi to call me, but I haven't heard from either one of them."

Will barely slowed to take the ramp to the interstate. "So, they don't know that Boyd may be in the area?"

"No."

Brad's cell phone rang, and he glanced at the ID. "It's the doctor," he said and answered. "Thanks for getting back with me, Doc. I'm putting you on speaker."

"I'm sorry I didn't get back to you earlier, but we've had an issue here." Stress echoed in the doctor's voice. "What's the problem?"

"I'm en route to your facility because I believe my sister is in

41

danger. A man who has been stalking her knows she's at Living Free."

"I see. Is this person capable of murder?"

Will gripped the steering wheel tighter. Boyd had gotten to Andi. He knew it in his bones.

"What's happened?" Brad demanded.

"One of our patients drowned yesterday, or at least that's what we thought. The local medical examiner did the autopsy this morning, and it turns out she had no water in her lungs. State Police are on their way."

"Do you know where my sister is?"

"I'm afraid not. It's free time, and everyone is scattered on the campus. But we have the staff locating all the patients because of the possible danger."

"How long is free time?" Will asked.

"It ends in thirty minutes, and group therapy sessions begin. I'll see if I can find her and call you back."

Why did Andi always attract danger? Will's heart couldn't take losing her. In the passenger seat, Brad's lips moved silently. Praying. That's what Will should be doing instead of worrying.

Silence rode with them while they waited for the call back. When it came, Brad answered on the first ring. "Is she all right?"

"I'm assuming so. She and one of the other patients, Mackenzie Knight, went jogging. I've sent someone to find them both."

Will shot a glance toward Brad. His face mirrored Will's fear. Information on Mackenzie Knight, aka Chloe Morgan, was the reason for Boyd's attack on Andi earlier in the week.

Revenge

CHAPTER ELEVEN

Jason waited in the woods just off the curve of the path, ready to jerk the clear plastic rope taut when the two women got even with him. He'd rather deal only with the reporter, but it looked as though they were a package deal.

With the binoculars he scanned toward the rehab facility to make sure no one else approached. Satisfied they were alone, he stuffed the field glasses in his backpack and then mentally ran through the takedown. Glock automatic in his waistband, the syringes with ketamine in his jacket. Once they were on the ground, he would take care of Hollister first then deal with the teenager. If she ran off, he still had time to get the reporter in his boat and get away.

If the girl hung around, then he'd take her as well. She was a looker, so that was a bonus and would fetch a good price from the Russian once Jason had her dark hair dyed blonde. He didn't know what it was about blondes, but they always fetched a higher price. Maybe the girl would even make the Russian forget about Chloe.

What was taking them so long to come back this way? He rubbed his nose where Andi Hollister had butted him. She would pay for that. Maybe instead of killing her, he'd sell her to the Russian, too.

It would be her worst nightmare.
***
Andi called to Chloe as they neared the gate at the edge of Living Free's property line. They had come out for another run and at least she wasn't as winded this time. "It's almost one-fifteen.

Time to head back."

The teenager slowed to a walk and when Andi caught up with her, Chloe nodded toward the forest to the right of the jogging path. "Who owns the property on the other side?"

"I don't know. With all the timber, maybe Weyerhaeuser. Not a place we want to trespass."

"You don't have to worry about that—it's creepy looking in there," Chloe said with a shudder. "You're not so winded today, and you don't seem to have any pain."

Andi paused. "You're right, I don't."

"Did you ever?"

What kind of question was that? "You think I'm making up my pain?"

Chloe shrugged. "It happens a lot with addicts."

She was not an addict. If she were, there wouldn't be a single Lortab left in her suitcase. But she couldn't tell Chloe that. "I had real pain when I took the pills."

Chloe studied her face, and Andi forced herself not to look away. Then the girl gave a small shrug. "Have you heard anything more about what happened to Roxie?"

Glad for the subject change, Andi said, "No, and I'm sorry you had to see that."

"I've seen dead people before. Do you think someone killed her?"

"Why would you ask that?" Andi figured suicide, but she shouldn't be surprised Chloe thought of murder—a subject that wouldn't cross the mind of most teens. But Chloe had lost her innocence long ago.

"I just have this feeling."

"Does your room face the lake?" Andi asked and continued when Chloe nodded. "Did you see anyone on the pier last night?"

"Before all that thunder and lightning?"

"No, during."

"I don't think I looked out. I don't like lightning." Chloe

cocked her head. "Did you see someone?"

"I thought I did, when lightning lit up the sky, but the next flash, no one was there. I probably just imagined it."

"Finding Roxie was enough to throw you off." The girl glanced toward the forest on their right and shivered. "Does this place creep you out?"

"The thought of snakes in there does." Andi glanced toward the dark and forbidding forest. She had to admit the skin on the back of her neck prickled when she looked toward it. "Try to think of it as Bambi's home."

"The home where her mother was killed? Gee, thanks."

"Don't always look on the dark side," she said. "Race you back to the pier?"

"You're on!"

Chloe took off like a shot and Andi scrambled to catch up. Ten yards separated them when Chloe went down. Before Andi had time to react, she stumbled, pitching forward. A man's hand clamped over her mouth, and she lashed out, kicking and elbowing him. She barely noticed the sting on her arm.

"What are you doing?" Chloe screamed.

"Run! Get help." Andi tried to pry his hands loose, but strength ebbed from her fingers.

Instead the girl jumped on Andi's attacker, flailing her fists against his body. He turned on Chloe, and Andi saw his face. Her heart sank. Jason Boyd!

She wanted to help Chloe, but her body refused to obey her mind. She couldn't even warn the girl about the needle he took from his jacket. It was as though she hovered over the scene as he wrestled Chloe to the ground and plunged the needle in her shoulder.

Her thoughts shifted through her mind like a kaleidoscope. Had to do something before Boyd dragged them away. Leave something. *The cross!* Andi fumbled in her pocket and pulled the key ring out, dropping it to the ground. With the toe of her shoe, she covered it with dead grass.

Will would find it. He would come for her. *Would he?* He'd washed his hands of her. She was on her own.

CHAPTER TWELVE

Will checked the speedometer. Eighty. Too fast for these winding roads. He eased his foot back to seventy and tamped down the anxiety that gripped him. Another half hour to go before they reached the rehab facility.

"She's going to be okay," Brad said.

"I wish I could be sure of that." What if she wasn't? She believed he didn't love her. The thought pained him. He had to save her. Why did she always have a way of getting into dangerous situations without even trying? He took his eyes from the road for a second and glanced at her brother. From the rigid set of his jaw, he was as worried as Will.

"Watch that deer!"

Will jerked his attention back to the road and braked, sending the Escape into a fishtail as a big buck raced across the highway. "Sorry about that," he said when he had the car under control.

"Slow it down a little. Won't do my sister any good if we don't get there."

He was right.

"Stop beating yourself up because you didn't look for a GPS tracker."

"But I should have." Will had no excuse. That should have been an automatic response when he discovered Jason Boyd was Andi's attacker. He'd just been so angry when he left the hospital, he hadn't thought at all.

Brad cleared his throat.

"What?"

"What happened with you and Andi? Last thing you told me was you'd bought a ring and then Andi tells me you broke it off."

If he thought changing the subject would help, this wasn't the topic to do it. "It's complicated," he said. Will couldn't tell him their relationship might be over.

"What's the problem?"

He gripped the steering wheel, focusing on the road. *Tell him. He knows his sister, he'll understand.*

"Are you interested in someone else?"

"No!" Will blew out a breath. "It's nothing like that."

He did not want to discuss his relationship with Andi right now. And no way was he going to tell anyone, especially Andi's brother, that when she did things like Monday night because of the drugs, it ripped his insides out. It was just like his mother abandoning him all over again because of her alcohol addiction.

Dumped on his aunt's doorstep when he was a baby, he'd been four or five when he realized his mother only showed up when she was out of money and had no other place to stay. It had taken him years to realize she wasn't rejecting him because of anything he'd done or not done. No, she rejected him because alcohol was more important. Still didn't take the sting out, and he'd made the decision to not give his heart to anyone on drugs. Not even Andi Hollister.

But life had a way of laughing at him. Otherwise he never would have fallen in love with Andi, and every time she took the pills or did something foolhardy because of them, it twisted the knife in his heart a little more.

"Look, Bro, Andi is going to kick the pills once and for all."

Brad knew him like a brother, for sure. Evidently even knew what he was thinking. "I hope so." He checked the time on the dash. "Call and see if they've located her."

A minute later, Brad said, "It's gone to voice mail. How far away are we?"

"Check the GPS on my phone."

Revenge

"Says here ten minutes."

Will pressed the accelerator. "Let's make eight."

In a little under eight minutes, they pulled into the long, winding drive to Living Free. Through the trees lining the lane, Will spotted flashing blue lights. Normally a good sign, but...

"I hope they don't try to keep us out of the search," Brad muttered.

He'd had the same thought as Will. This wasn't their jurisdiction. "I'd hoped we would get here first."

Will parked beside one of the patrol cars and climbed out of his car. A half dozen deputy sheriffs surrounded a small woman he recognized as Doctor Sullivan, and they were looking at a map spread on the hood of one of the squad cars. It'd been a few years since he'd seen her, but she hadn't changed much. Except he'd never seen her in jeans and boots.

She spied them and broke away from the officers. "Thank goodness you're here," she said, shaking Brad's hand. "We haven't been able to locate your sister or Mackenzie Knight."

"Where were they last seen?" Will asked.

She turned to him. "Will Kincade, is that you?"

"Yes. It's good to see you again," he said, surprised she remembered him. Unlike Brad, who had taken several classes with the doctor, he and the doctor had taken only one class together in college. "We'd like to go to the area where Andi and Mackenzie were last seen."

"Of course." She turned to the deputies. "Sheriff Boggan, could I have a word with you?"

The man who detached himself stood a head taller than any of the others. When he reached them, Lillian made the introductions.

Will shook the outstretched hand that engulfed his. The man surely played professional basketball. "I hope you don't mind if we help you search."

"What's your connection?" the sheriff asked.

"I'm Andi Hollister's brother," Brad said.

"And..." Will squared his shoulders. "We're going to be married."

Boggan nodded. "As long as you remember I'm in charge, we won't have any problems." He folded his arms across his chest. "We have to consider the two may have decided to leave—it wouldn't be the first time a patient decided they didn't want to stay. I have a deputy driving the road to town looking for them."

Will glanced toward the parking lot and found Andi's Corolla. "Her car is still here, so I don't think she left. At least not willingly."

"We'll see." The sheriff turned to the doctor. "You want to show us the jogging trail where they were last seen?"

Doctor Sullivan led them to a dirt path near the lake. "This is where almost everyone jogs or walks."

"How far does the path go?" Brad asked.

"It ends at our property line, about half a mile."

Will addressed the sheriff. "How do you want to handle this?"

"Why don't you come with me and a couple of my men? We'll cover the path as far as it goes. See if there's any sign the women have been on it. Everybody have gloves?" When they nodded, he turned to the director. "Doctor Sullivan, you want to join us? Or search elsewhere?"

"I'll come with you."

Doctor Sullivan walked with the other deputies as they fanned out while Will and Brad searched on either side of the path. To his right, he overheard the sheriff contact his man searching the road into town. "Keep looking," he said. "I figure you'll find them before we do."

Will balled his hands. He was wrong. Andi made a commitment to stay two weeks and she wouldn't break it. A shiny object caught his eye and he knelt and picked it up. A drink tab. He kept walking and searching, kicking the grass occasionally.

"Doesn't look like they've been here," the sheriff said.

Revenge

"We're not to the end of the path," Will replied. Part of him hoped she had left. Running away he could deal with. Being captured by Boyd…

A pile of leaves looked freshly disturbed. His heart kicked up a notch. Will knelt and sifted through the leaves. When he leaned over to examine the grass around the pile, the sunlight glinted on something silvery. He pulled it from the grass. The key ring with the silver cross he'd given Andi.

He stood, waving the key ring. "Andi was here!"

CHAPTER THIRTEEN

"You're a little spitfire, aren't you?" Jason held the girl down until the ketamine took effect and he could get them into the woods. Something about the girl was familiar. Then he realized her eyes reminded him just a little of Chloe. But then, several teenage girls had reminded him of her. Once she relaxed, he secured her hands with a zip tie and took the automatic from his waistband, pointing it at them. "Okay, ladies, let's move."

He'd used ketamine before, liked the way it made his victims compliant and incapacitated, yet able to walk. Beat having to carry both to the boat docked a good half-mile away. It took twenty minutes to reach the boat and once aboard, he secured them with another zip tie from their hands to a metal bar—just in case the ketamine wore off.

Jason headed the boat out of the inlet. He'd left his SUV at a public launch five miles up the river. From there he would take them to the vacant cabin he'd found. It was the perfect spot to get the information from Hollister about Chloe. He glanced back at the girl. If Hollister didn't cooperate, he'd use the girl to put pressure on the reporter.

In the distance, a boat appeared on the lake. In the three days he'd watched the rehab, he hadn't seen one boat enter the inlet. Boyd fished his binoculars from the backpack and zoomed in on the fast approaching boat. Four men. His heart shifted into overdrive when he recognized one of them. Razor.

How did he find him? *His cell phone!*

They'd spotted him and were angling across the water in a boat twice the size of his little ski boat. He couldn't outrun them. Jason swung the boat around and raced toward the shore. His only hope was to get into the forest and hike back to his SUV.

The question was, did he want to take his captives with him? Yes. Andi Hollister was his leverage. Even if she didn't know where

Chloe was, the Russian thought she did. If it came down to it, he'd trade her life for his in a heartbeat.

A bullet whizzed past him and pierced the windshield. He raised the binoculars once more. One of the men, not Razor, aimed a rifle at the boat. Had to be high-powered as far away as they were. Jason swung the boat in an arc, almost capsizing it, but the bullet missed and split the water. He gauged the distance the other boat was to them. He had maybe ten minutes to get the women off the boat and disappear into the forest. Had to do something to buy time.

As Jason guided the boat to where he'd tethered it earlier, he grabbed a half-full gas can he'd stashed in case he needed the extra fuel. Not as much as he'd like, but it'd be enough to do the job. He planned to empty the gasoline along the grassy edge. It'd been a dry fall and the grass was dry, even after the storm last night. Should make a nice fire.

CHAPTER FOURTEEN

Andi's world spun out of control and she shook her head to clear it. What were they doing in a boat driven by Jason Boyd? Her gaze slid to the windshield. *A bullet hole.* She *had* heard bullets. Friend or foe? Anyone would be better than Boyd.

Where were they? Then she remembered the sting. He'd drugged them. Probably with one of the date rape drugs that would allow them to stay on their feet and walk without giving Boyd any trouble.

Beside her, Chloe stirred. Andi's hands were secured with a zip tie, but not so tightly that she couldn't twist them back and forth. Another cable tie anchored her to the boat. She lifted her hands as high she could and made a "shhh" motion even though the girl couldn't hear her. But she understood and nodded.

She had to get Chloe off the boat and away from Jason. Did he know who Chloe was? No. If he did, Andi would be dead. Like Roxie. He must have mistaken Roxie for her yesterday. Her stomach rolled at the thought, and she almost lost it.

The boat rammed the shore, throwing them both forward. Then Jason jumped off the boat with the gas can. Almost immediately the odor of gasoline burned her nose. What was he doing? Was he going to set them on fire?

A quick scan of the boat revealed an oar beside the seat. Andi jerked on the cable tie securing her to the boat, burning her wrists.

Revenge

Maybe if she turned the tie to where it locked, she could break free. Once she had it in place, she jerked again and it snapped free.

Jason was busy emptying the gas can, and she grabbed the oar and stood. Everything whirled and she staggered. No! She had to do keep her balance and focused on the bank, managing get closer to him. He turned, ducking just as she brought the oar down.

He grabbed the end of the oar and jerked it out of her hands. "Don't be stupid! Listen to me and listen good," he said. "Those bullets you heard? The men firing at us are ten times worse than me. If they get you, you and your little friend here will be sold to the highest bidder. If they don't kill you outright. Now get back on the boat."

Andi snapped her gaze to the men headed their way. Jason was bad, but at least there was only one of him. She couldn't let them get Chloe. She climbed back on the boat, conscious of the gun Jason held. Once they both were aboard, Jason pointed for her to sit beside Chloe.

Keeping his gun trained on them, he backed the boat out, and wheeled it around. Then he sliced the zip tie securing Chloe to the boat. "Jump out," he ordered.

Five seconds later he gunned the motor and then jumped after them. While they splashed toward the bank, the boat headed straight toward the other vessel. Once they reached shore, Jason held the pistol on them as he grabbed a handful of dry grass and handed it to Andi with a lighter. "Set it on fire and then toss it."

She did what he said and jumped back as the grass lit with a whoosh.

"Let's go!" He herded them toward the forest. "You want to live, stay close to me. I know a cave not far away we can hide in."

Andi looked over her shoulder. The grass fire was quickly spreading.

"Move!"

Andi's gaze collided with Chloe's and she nodded for the girl to do what Jason said. They had no choice.

CHAPTER FIFTEEN

The sheriff hurried to see what Will had found. "You're sure that belongs to one of them?" he asked.

"Yes," Will said. "I gave this to her a couple of months ago."

The sheriff scanned the ground. "See if you can find anything else or which way they went from here."

They searched the area, and suddenly Brad yelled. "Over here. Looks like a syringe."

Will's hopes plummeted. A syringe meant they'd probably been injected with a drug that would make them manageable but still able to walk. While the sheriff bagged the needle, Will shaded his eyes and scanned the lake. Was that smoke curling toward the sky?

"Fire!" A deputy pointed toward the bend in the lake.

Will froze. What if Andi was trapped there?

"No!" Doctor Sullivan jerked her phone out, punching in numbers. "It's so dry, the whole place will go up like a tinderbox."

Will ran toward the fire. When he rounded the curve, he braked to a halt. Flames engulfed the dry grass on the bank and raced toward the forest, eating up the underbrush. What if Andi was caught in that inferno?

Brad caught up to him. "What's wrong with that boat?"

Will turned to see what he was talking about. A boat circled in a tight ring on the lake. Maybe she was on it. "Can you tell if anyone is onboard?"

Revenge

"Too far, but I don't think the boat would be circling like that if anyone was on it."

"What the blue blazes—" Sheriff Boggan "We need to get a fire brigade going!"

"Can you get someone here to check out that boat?" Will pointed toward the lake. "The women could be stowed aboard."

"On it."

Doctor Sullivan jogged toward them. "Called the forestry service but they'd already spotted the smoke. They had a crew cutting underbrush a couple of miles from here," she said, pointing to the green fire truck and crew truck fast approaching. "More firefighters should be here soon."

In seconds men spilled out of the crew truck with their Pulaskis and chainsaws. Will and Brad backed off from the fire, getting out of the way of the professionals. Will checked with the sheriff about the boat that still turned in a circle.

"Should be someone here any minute," Boggan said. "The county is sending a fire boat along with more personnel. They'll check it out."

As he spoke, a jet ski with two people on it entered the mouth of the lake and zoomed toward the boat. Will held his breath as the man nosed into the boat and the second person jumped aboard. In seconds the boat headed to shore. When they were close enough, he yelled, "Anybody on board?"

"Nope," the deputy yelled back before he turned the boat toward the pier near the rehab.

Will pulled Brad aside. "If they're not on the boat, then he must have taken them into the woods. I'm going to look for them. You in?"

"I'm in. If we stay west of the fire, we should be okay," Brad said.

Will thought about not telling Boggan, but once they were missed, he might think he needed to send in a rescue team. "Sheriff," he said. "You don't need us here. We're going to see if we can find signs of where Boyd took Andi and the girl."

Boggan shook his head.

Before he could say no, Will said, "You're tied up here. If we don't find them soon, he may kill them. And don't worry, we'll stay clear of the fire."

Boggan hesitated, and then he turned to a deputy. "Get me two radios and a satellite communicator. And a couple of canteens of water." When the deputy returned with them, the sheriff said, "Keep in touch and if you find their trail, let me know. The radio will give us voice contact if you don't go too far inland. After that use the GPS unit to message. It'll give us your location at all times, as well. And watch the fire. It could change direction anytime."

Will was glad for the equipment. He didn't know how well his cell phone would work in the dense trees. Once Boggan gave them a quick tutorial on the GPS unit, Will nodded to Brad. "Ready?"

"Yeah," Brad said. "Let's spread out a little, but stay in each other's line of vision."

Inside the forest, Will scoured the area while he kept one eye on the direction of the fire. He and Brad had worked for the forestry service when they were teenagers, and the sheriff didn't have to tell him how quickly a fire could turn.

Will figured Boyd wasn't stupid, either. He would stay behind the fire line as well. Methodically, he worked the undergrowth with Brad to his left, searching for broken branches, kicked up leaves, and footprints in the undergrowth, although as dry as it'd been, he doubted there would be prints.

"You see anything?" he called to Brad.

"Maybe." Brad's voice held hesitancy. "A couple of broken twigs and one limb stripped bare. Recently, too."

Will abandoned his grid and hurried to where Brad waited and examined the broken branch. Definitely a fresh break. "Do you see anymore?" he asked, turning in a circle. Ten yards straight ahead the top half of a frond had been stripped clean. "There," he yelled.

"Andi is marking their way."

Will's radio crackled and then the sheriff spoke, "Detective Kincade, can you hear me?"

"Loud and clear," Will said.

"Another boat has been discovered a little farther up the lake with one man aboard. A cabin cruiser. Claims he's just fishing and allowed the deputy to search his boat. No sign of the women."

"You think it could be more than that?"

"It's hard to tell. Big boat for just one person to be fishing. He didn't hang around."

"Thanks," Will said. "We're well west of the fire and found signs someone had been through here. We'll keep you up to date."

"Do you need assistance?"

"Could always use help."

"I'll send my deputies as soon as I can cut them loose here."

The radio went silent and Will exchanged glances with Brad. "You think the boat circling the lake belongs to Boyd?"

"Yeah," Brad replied. "But why didn't he didn't use it to transport Andi and Chloe wherever he's going instead of hiking through these woods?"

Will rubbed the back of his neck. "What if there was more than one person on the cabin cruiser, and they tracked Boyd to the area? If it's someone he's been in contact with on his phone, they could pretty well pinpoint where he was. Or maybe they have one of these things and it connected to Boyd's phone." He held up the radio then glanced in the direction of the fire. "And maybe that's why he set the fire."

Brad nodded. "To keep the other boat from docking and following them."

"Yeah. They'd have to find another place to come ashore."

"So the guy on the boat dropped them and was waiting around to pick them up when the deputy scared him off."

Will scanned the area. "That means they're probably somewhere in these woods."

CHAPTER SIXTEEN

Andi made sure she stayed between Jason and Chloe as they hiked to the cave. Her feet hurt, her arms bled where briars had ripped the skin on her arms, and her wrists burned where the zip tie rubbed them, but at least her back wasn't hurting. And thankfully whatever he'd injected them with had worn off. She licked her dry lips and would give anything for a drink of water. "How much farther?" she asked.

"Just keep moving." Then Jason stopped and cocked his head. "Hold up a minute."

She and Chloe stopped. The forest was quiet, too quiet. Then she heard someone tromping through the brush. From the sound it was more than one person.

Jason wheeled around. "We have to hurry. They're not far behind us."

Andi stared at him, unable to move. Were they tracking them with the trail of broken branches and stripped leaves she'd left?

He shoved her. "Move!"

She snapped out of her daze. "Which way?"

He pointed to a ravine. "Across that and halfway up the hill to the cave."

Andi scanned the cliff. "I don't see a cave."

"It's there, so get moving unless you want Razor to take you with him."

Andi didn't want that. "We could go faster if you'd untie our hands."

"You're doing just fine. It's not much farther."

They half ran, half fell down the ravine to the small creek that ran through it. After jumping across it and they scrambled up the hill. Having their hands bound made using the vines and saplings to pull themselves along much harder.

Near the top, Jason pointed to a large pine branch. "Move that brush."

She and Chloe tugged it away, revealing the mouth of the cave. How long had he been watching her? Evidently long enough to plan out an escape route.

"Get inside."

Chloe hesitated. "It's...d-dark in there."

Andi agreed. "What if there are bears?"

"No matter what's in the cave, it's better than what's out here. *Move!*"

Andi crawled in first, noticing right away the damp, earthy scent. She found the wall and scooted back against it as Chloe climbed in beside her. The girl had said little. Probably afraid she'd say something that might give her away to Jason.

While Boyd struggled with getting the limb over the opening, Andi checked to see how far back the cave went. It disappeared into darkness a few yards from where they sat. Did she want to risk getting trapped? Or falling to her death? No. There had to be another way to escape Boyd.

"What are we going to do?" Chloe whispered.

It was the first opportunity they'd had to talk. "Follow my lead."

"No talking in there," Jason hissed.

Andi squeezed Chloe's hand. Somehow they had to get the jump on him. But not until the danger from the other men had passed. She tried once more to assess the depth of the cave, but it was impossible, especially now that Jason had blocked the opening with the brush, plunging them into near darkness.

He crawled inside and sat across from them. "If we're lucky, they'll think we went to the road at the top of the cliff."

There was a road? If they could get away from Jason and make it to the road, there had to be people looking for them by now. Surely they'd check the surrounding roads.

The small amount of light that filtered through the pine branches allowed her to make out Jason's outline. Voices reached them. Andi frowned. They weren't speaking English. The voices came closer and she shifted, trying to hear what they were saying.

"Don't move," Jason whispered.

Suddenly they came into view. There were three of them and they carried rifles. One of the men stopped near the mouth of the cave, just feet from them. What if he saw the fresh cut on the tree limb covering it? Andi held her breath as Jason tensed and lifted his automatic. One of the other men shouted something she couldn't understand.

"Nav," the man outside the cave answered, shaking his head, and then he moved past the opening.

That she understood. Whatever the questions was, the answer was no. Their voices soon faded. Unless the men doubled back, they should be safe. From them, anyway.

Minutes ticked off. Jason turned and kept the gun trained on her and Chloe. With his other hand, he cautioned them to remain quiet. Probably wanted to give the men time to clear the area. She shifted against the cold ground and smothered a groan. With adrenaline no longer pumping through her, every muscle in Andi's body ached. She'd kill for a Lortab.

The thought brought her up short, and she pushed it to the back of her mind. Except it didn't stay there. She rolled her shoulders, trying to loosen the knots, and the desire for one of the yellow tablets grew. Something to give her a boost.

"What's the girl's name?" Jason asked.

His voice made Andi jump and beside her, Chloe stiffen.

Andi couldn't believe he had no clue. She rubbed her thumb across her knuckles, stalling, and he nudged her with the pistol.

"Mackenzie," Andi said. "What are you going to do with us?"

"Depends on what you tell me."

Her heart sank.

"Where's Chloe?"

"Nothing's changed since Monday night—I don't know."

"I didn't believe you then and I don't believe you now." He grabbed Chloe by the arm and dragged her beside him. "If you don't tell me right now, your friend will die."

Andi's mouth dried. Either way, Chloe would lose.

"One."

Chloe whimpered and tried to pull away from him. He jerked her back.

"Two."

"She's in rehab!" The words shot out of Andi's mouth.

"Where?" Jason demanded.

Andi frowned. The air in the cave seemed different. She sniffed, trying to decide what had changed. Smoke! She smelled smoke. "The fire! It's coming this way!"

"No!" Chloe screamed.

"What are you talking about?" he asked.

"Smoke! Can't you smell it?" It was coming from deep within the cave. "We have to get out of here."

CHAPTER SEVENTEEN

Will stopped by a tiny stream of water and scanned the brush for broken branches. They had moved into a hardwood section of the forest, and with most of the leaves carpeting the forest floor, they had a better view of the area. The fire also had more fuel.

Why had Andi quit leaving a trail? "Do you see anything?" he shouted to Brad.

"Nothing over here, but it looks like they are headed right into the path of the fire." Brad knelt and wet his handkerchief.

Will did the same. If the smoke got too thick, the wet cloth would help. Everything inside him said he had to get to Andi.

Brad joined him. "Which way do you think they went?"

He wished he had a map of the area. It was plain Jason was working his way to *somewhere*, and Will figured it would be near a road. Where were the reinforcements Boggan promised?

"You hear that?" Brad asked.

Will cocked his ear. "Sounds like people coming this way from the fire, so it's not Boggan's deputies."

"Maybe it's Jason with Andi and Chloe. They might've run into the fire line and are doubling back."

Brad and Will drew their guns and waited. Three men carrying rifles topped the ridge, but instead of coming down into the valley, they walked the backbone of the ridge. Suddenly one of them shouted something Will didn't understand, and then they disappeared on the other side of the ridge.

They must have seen Jason and the women. He nodded for Brad to follow him. They had to get to Andi and Chloe before those men caught up with them.

CHAPTER EIGHTEEN

Andi watched for an opportunity to escape as Jason scrambled out of the cave and pushed the branch away, but there was no way to get away from him without getting shot. Immediately, the odor of smoke became stronger. He cursed.

"We'll have to make a run for the lake," he said, pulling Chloe to him. "If you try to escape, I'll shoot her."

Andi nodded. "Don't hurt her."

"That'll be up to you. Let's go!"

Andi stumbled out of the cave into the hazy smoke that filled the hills and valleys. She looked over her shoulder. She couldn't see the fire, but the roar in the trees overhead was unmistakable. It was coming their way.

She followed Jason as he half dragged Chloe down the hill. They reached the creek in the ravine, and when Jason jumped across, his foot caught on the root of a birch tree. He screamed and went down, pulling Chloe with him. When Andi reached them, he didn't have the gun in his hand. Instead he clutched his leg, moaning.

She scanned the ground for the gun and found it several yards from where he'd fallen, and she scooped it up.

"Help me," Jason cried. "My leg is broken."

Help him? She ought to shoot him. Andi pulled Chloe up from where she'd fallen. "Are you okay?"

She dusted the dirt from her knees. "Yeah."

"Let's go."

"You can't leave me!"

Andi stared at him. The man had tried to kill her, had pimped Chloe out, had kidnapped them, killed Roxie and now he expected them to help him? Getting revenge was so tempting. She eyed him. He was at least six-one and weighed close to two hundred pounds. How would she and Chloe handle him?

Somewhere behind them, a tree crashed to the ground with a whomp. She couldn't leave him to die in the fire, either. "Do you have a knife?"

Wariness flashed in his eyes. "Why?"

"The two of us can't get you out of here. We need something for you to lean on."

Indecision played across his face, then he nodded and pulled a bone-handled knife from his pocket. "It may be too small."

He pressed a silver button and a skinny blade flipped out. Andi shuddered. Was it the one he'd used on the homeless man at Tom Lee Park? She shoved the thought away and took the knife, quickly cutting the zip ties around Chloe's wrists and then handed her the knife.

Once Andi's hands were free, she and Chloe helped Jason pull himself to the birch tree that had tripped him. Then she found a sapling a couple of inches in diameter. She hadn't been a Girl Scout and getting it down was slow progress with the small knife. Soon her hand cramped from hacking at the tree.

"Let me try it a while," Chloe said.

She attacked the other side, making long angled cuts all around the trunk. Soon they had it freed and quickly fashioned a makeshift crutch. When they returned to where Jason lay, he held a syringe in his hand.

"What are you doing?" Andi demanded.

"Ketamine," he replied, and then shrugged. "I had an extra one, just in case one of the others failed."

"You—" Andi fisted her hands and tamped down the rage

that threatened to close her throat. They were lucky he hadn't killed them with the drug. She grabbed the crutch from Chloe and threw it down beside him. "We're out of here."

"You can't leave me."

"Oh, yes we can. You have that," she said, pointing to the crutch. Then she grabbed Chloe by the hand. "Let's go."

"It wasn't personal," Jason yelled. "Hey! I have a couple of oxycodones if you want one."

He had pain pills? Andi licked her lips and hesitated. Just one would get her back to the rehab facility.

"I just wanted to know where Chloe is."

Beside her, Chloe turned around. "Why? Why do you want to know that?"

"The Russian wants her. They'll kill me if I don't find her." He struggled to stand.

A shot rang out, and Jason crumpled to the ground. Andi jerked her head around. The men! She grabbed Chloe's hand and pulled her behind the tree. "We have to make a run for it."

The oxycodones. They were in Jason's pocket. It wouldn't take a second to get them. She peeked around the tree. The men were still a good ways from them, and she inched around the tree, not worried about them shooting—they wanted her alive. Jason lay just a few feet from the tree.

"What are you doing?" Chloe yelled.

Andi stared at the girl, her heart pounding against her chest. In a flash, she knew exactly what she was doing. What any addict would do. The thought sickened her. "I..." she closed her eyes, trying to shut out the truth.

A bullet split the bark above her head, jerking her back to reality. "I'm sorry. Run for that tree!" Andi pointed to a nearby tree that looked like it could hide them and grabbed Chloe's hand. "And stay low."

"Andi!"

Will? She looked over her shoulder. She could still see the

Revenge

three men, but smoke had settled on the tree line above them. She might not be able to see Will, but she knew his voice anywhere. He'd come for her. And if he was here, maybe her brother was too.

Andi wanted to yell and let him know where they were, but it would alert the other men as well. His voice had come from behind them—he and Brad must have followed the trail she left.

Gunfire peppered the air.

"Run," Andi cried. If they could find a place to hide…

She pulled Chloe with her, ignoring the branches that slapped her in the face. Another round of gunfire rang out, but it didn't seem to be coming their way.

She ran until pain stabbed her lungs. It was so hard to breathe, and she covered her hand to muffle her cough. Where were they? Were they going the right way? Andi stopped and they rested against another oak tree. She was so thirsty. If only she'd taken time to get a drink of water from the creek.

"Are we lost?" Chloe choked out.

"No. As long as we keep moving away from the fire, we'll eventually come to the lake." She hoped. "Do you see any signs that this is where we came through earlier?"

The teenager shook her head. "Maybe if we found another cave."

"Then we'd be trapped by the fire." She glanced at the girl. Tears streaked her sooty face, but she was a trooper. "We're going to get out of here. Will and maybe my brother are already in the woods, looking for us."

At least she hoped they were, that it really was Will calling her name. But what if she imagined it? Andi pushed off from the tree. "We better keep moving. Shoot for that pine over there."

Just as they reached the tree, arms like steel wrapped around Andi's shoulders, pinning her arms to her body. She kicked and bucked against the man, twisting, trying to get loose.

He gripped her wrist and then her elbow squeezing her pressure points. Her arm went limp then she felt a sharp blow to her neck, and white light exploded in her brain before darkness flooded her consciousness.

***

Will doubted Andi had heard his scream. He drew his pistol and fired at the men, even though they were out of range. They scattered and Will and Brad scrambled down the hill. When they reached the creek, Boyd lay on the ground. Will knelt and felt his neck. No pulse. He shook his head and pointed up the next hill where they'd last seen the men. Brad nodded and they struck out. The climb wasn't as steep as the one they'd just come down, but Will felt as though he had a target on his chest.

Where did the men go? Half way up the ridge he found out when a bullet slammed into a tree inches above his head. Will ducked behind the tree. He looked for Brad. He'd found another tree.

Will dropped to the ground and crawled through the underbrush. Dirt kicked up a yard from his position. Will rolled and found another sturdy oak to hide behind. How had the man seen him? *A scope.* Must not be the best shot in the world, but even bad shooters got lucky sometimes. They had to get the drop on him. But first he needed to send a message to Boggan and took out the GPS unit.

Tracking three armed men. They're after Andi and girl. Send help. STAT.

Seconds later, a message popped up. *Sending men. See your location.*

"Boggan's sending reinforcements."

"Good," Brad grunted. "Do you see the other two men?"

Will scanned the area. "No. They probably went after Andi and Chloe. How much ammo you got?"

"Full magazine in my gun. Another one on my belt."

About what Will had. "Draw his attention. I'm going to try and get behind him."

When Brad let loose with a burst of gunfire, Will dashed to another tree. The shooter fired back, letting Will pinpoint his

Revenge

position. Then brush rustled. The man was on the move, but where did he go? Minutes passed as Will waited for him to fire again.

Brad dashed to another tree, drawing the shooter's fire. With the man in his line of vision, Will adjusted his direction until he was within twenty feet of the man. When he lifted his rifle again, Will shouted, "Police. Drop your rifle!"

The man swung the gun toward Will.

CHAPTER NINETEEN

When Andi came to, her head dangled from a man's shoulder as he carried her fireman style through the woods. Had she dreamed Will called her name? Smoke burned her nose, and she coughed. At the same time she kicked against the man, and he swung her down like she weighed nothing.

When he said something in what sounded like Russian, she remembered Jason talked about someone named Razor who worked for the Russian. Then the man carrying Chloe dumped her on the ground and pulled a knife from the scabbard on his belt. He laid it against Chloe's neck.

Andi struggled to get loose. "No! You can't—"

The man restraining Andi spun her around. His face was hard, and a scar in one eyebrow gave it a perpetual lift. His ice blue eyes held no compassion. "Then you must cooperate."

These men had killed Jason. She couldn't let them hurt Chloe. *Play along with them.* "You must be Razor. Take the knife away from her if you want me to cooperate."

She didn't think it was possible for his eyes to grow colder, but they did.

He gave the other man a curt nod and he moved the knife. "So Jason talked about me. He shouldn't have done that. Where is Chloe Morgan?"

"I don't know."

He backhanded Andi, ringing her ears. "Once more, where is Chloe Morgan?"

"I don't know, I told you!"

He hit her again, knocking her to the ground.

Chloe scrambled to her side. "Stop! Don't hurt her again! I—"

"Why do you want Chloe so bad?" Andi raised her voice to drown out anything Chloe might have said.

Gunfire volleyed behind them, and Razor jerked his head toward the sound. Then he lifted the girl like she weighed nothing and set her on her feet. "We will finish this discussion later. Now move."

Will. She hadn't dreamed it! Andi looked over her shoulder as more gunfire erupted.

"Whoever it is will not get here in time. Walk where I tell you, or my friend Yuri will dispose of your friend. I do not need her." He glared at her. "Do you understand? I need only you."

Yeah, until she told him what he wanted to know, but she nodded. "Then turn her loose."

His lip curled and he laughed. "No. For now she's my leverage with you." Then he lifted Chloe's chin and turned her face from side to side. "Besides, she has the look my customers like and will bring a good price. Even more than you."

So he didn't plan on killing them. She sneaked a look at Chloe. Her chin quivered in his hand and her body stood rigid. Andi could only imagine what was going through the girl's mind.

God, help us. The prayer was late—Andi should have been talking to God all along. But she'd been too intent on taking care of this herself. And if she hadn't wasted precious seconds after Jason was shot thinking about the drugs he had, maybe they could have gotten away.

Razor shoved Chloe toward Yuri and then prodded Andi to follow. "Start walking."

Andi's throat was parched and she figured Chloe's was too. "Do you have any water?"

"Do I look like I have water? Move on. You can get it at the next creek we cross."

They walked for what seemed like forever. She dragged her feet when she could to leave a trail for Will to follow. The other man and Razor talked between themselves in what sounded like Russian, and every so often he studied a small hand-held radio, and then changed direction. Once he sent a message to someone. Probably someone on the boat she'd seen. She and Chloe had to get away before they got to the lake.

She hadn't heard any more gunshots. If it had been Will and Brad doing the shooting, why hadn't they caught up with them?

***

Center mass. The thought flew through Will's mind. He fired his pistol as he dove to the ground and rolled. A bullet whizzed past his head. He hadn't missed. He couldn't have.

Brad ran toward the man as he stumbled to his knees, blood spreading across his chest. But he still held the rifle pointed straight at Will. His heart thudded against his chest as he stared down the barrel of the rifle. The sounds of the forest receded. Brad fired just as the shooter pulled the trigger.

Click.

The rifle misfired and the shooter pitched forward. Will scrambled to get to him. He kicked the rifle out of reach and turned the man over. Dead.

"You okay?" Brad asked when he reached Will.

"Yeah. Thanks. But he won't be able to help us find Andi."

Brad searched the dead man's pockets. "Maybe we can find them with this," he said, unclipping the carabiner on the man's belt and holding up a GPS. "This one looks more sophisticated than ours."

They powered the unit up and a map popped up. "This red line," Will said, pointing to a line that led from where they were to a point on the lake, "probably ends at the boat. And these two dots must be the other two men."

"Looks like they're about half a mile away."

Will tapped a message to Boggan on their GPS.

Revenge

Locate boat. Men headed toward it.

Boggan's reply came back almost immediately. *Do you have coordinates?*

Will looked up at Brad. "He wants the boat coordinates."

"Click on the boat. See if the map gives them."

Will tapped the screen were the red line ended and the coordinates popped up. He typed them in and sent it to Boggan.

Ten-four.

A message popped up on the dead man's GPS.

"What do you suppose it says?" Will asked as he stared at the foreign-spelled words.

"Not a clue."

"Then we better not answer it."

Will hooked the carabiner to his belt where he could still hold the unit in his hand. "Let's go find them."

They followed the red line to the top of the next ridge and Will scanned the area, searching for movement. At least the smoke haze wasn't as bad here. The GPS showed the men and their captives weren't that far away, maybe a quarter of a mile. He figured with just him and Brad, they'd been able to travel faster. He glanced at the unit and the system blinked and shut down. Will groaned and showed Brad the screen. "They must have figured out we had their GPS unit," he said.

A message appeared on the unit Boggan had given them.

Either coordinates are wrong or the boat moved.

CHAPTER TWENTY

Plans raced through Andi's mind with each step she took. That had been Will's voice she'd heard call her name, and Brad was sure to be with him. What if the man who stayed behind had killed them? No. She wouldn't accept that. If he'd accomplished his mission, he would have caught up with them by now. That meant Will and her brother were somewhere behind them. She needed to stall for time.

Halfway up the next ridge, Andi sank to the ground. "I can't go another step."

"You would prefer to be carried like before?"

He would do it, too. If she couldn't slow them down, then she had to devise a plan for Chloe to get away. Andi would not let her be sold into slavery again. If Chloe escaped, it would free Andi to take risks she otherwise couldn't. "No. But I have to go to the bathroom before we go farther."

"So do I," Chloe said.

Razor palmed his hands. "So, go."

"How about a little privacy." Andi crossed her arms. "It's not like we can get away from you."

"Americans." He spit on the ground. "So delicate."

The other man said something she didn't understand and Razor grunted. "All right. We will turn around."

"Can we not get behind the tree?"

He rolled his eyes. "Go. But be quick."

Revenge

Andi grabbed Chloe by the hand and they hurried to a forked oak tree several yards away. "I believe Will and Brad are behind us. I'm going to create a diversion when we get to the top of hill," she said, keeping her voice low. "And when I do, you run the way we just came for all you're worth."

"No talking!"

She'd hoped Razor hadn't heard her. "She's crying, and I'm just comforting her."

On cue, Chloe let out a bawl.

"Just be quick."

Andi patted the girl on her back. "Did you understand what I said?"

"I don't want to leave you."

"You have to. Will and Brad are somewhere behind us." She believed with all her heart that they hadn't been killed. "Find them."

Chloe nodded. "I've been listening to them talk and they're taking us to the boat."

"You understand Russian?"

"It's not Russian, it's Latvian. My grandparents—that's all they spoke."

"Time's up," Razor barked. "I'm coming to get you."

"Do what I said," Andi mouthed.

When they resumed hiking, Andi climbed as slowly as she dared to the top of the hill, praying it wouldn't reveal the lake. No. Just another ridge to climb once they descended the bluff where they stood, but at least the hills were getting smaller. She glanced over her shoulder, searching for a sign of Will. Her heart sank when there was no movement behind them.

Razor barely let them catch their breath before prodding them on. Yuri took the lead again, and Andi moved in behind him, hoping Razor wouldn't stop her from changing places with Chloe in their single file formation. When they came to an outcropping of rocks, Yuri easily hopped down from the first boulder.

It was now or never. Her heart beat against her ribs, and Andi hesitated. Then she jumped, tucking her body in a ball and crashed into Yuri. He tumbled forward. Andi caught herself and jumped up and charged down the hill. Behind her, Razor cursed and rocks skittered past her as he scrambled on the rocks to catch her.

For a second, Andi thought she would outrun him, but he was too fast for her. He tackled her at the base of the rocks and they tumbled against a tree. When he got his footing, he jerked her up. "I should kill you for this."

"Your boss probably wouldn't like that."

Yuri yelled something she didn't understand, and Razor wheeled around and a string of words flew from his mouth. Andi looked for Chloe. *Yes!* It worked. She'd gotten away.

When Yuri asked him a question, Razor flipped his hand and shook his head before he turned back to Andi. "The only way she can go is toward the fire. Your little trick will cost your friend her life."

"No, she'll make it," Andi said defiantly.

His lip curled. "Even if she does, it won't help you."

Revenge

CHAPTER TWENTY-ONE

They had spread out and Will called out to Brad, "Do you see any signs they've passed through here?"

"Not since the leaves that were kicked up."

That had been at least fifteen minutes ago. What if they were going the wrong way? What if he couldn't save Andi? A weight settled in his heart. He shook the thought off. He couldn't think that way.

"Something's coming this way," Brad yelled.

Will ducked behind a tree and waited until a small figure came in sight. "Chloe!"

She stopped and looked in their direction. Will stepped from behind the tree, and she ran to him.

"They have Andi!" she sobbed as she fell into his arm.

"How far ahead are they?" Will asked.

"I don't know. We came to some rocks, and Andi fell so I could get away. I don't know how long ago that's been. I just ran and ran." She straightened up. "But I broke branches so you could find her."

Brad ran to where they were. "How many men?"

"Two," she said. "Yuri and Razor—he's the boss."

"Have you ever seen them before?" Will asked.

"Not Yuri." Chloe sucked in a breath. "Razor came to Jason's house one time." Suddenly she halted. "Jason. Is he dead?"

"Yes." The relief that washed over her face seared Will's heart.

"Then he can't hurt me anymore."

"No, he can't."

"Do you know where they are taking Andi?" Brad asked.

"To a boat."

"That's what I was afraid of," Will said.

"Too bad we don't know its location."

"I might," Chloe said.

"What? How?"

"They were talking in Latvian and didn't know I could understand them. They talked about this boat."

"Did they say where it is?"

"Some place called Indian Creek."

Will looked at the GPS map. Indian Creek wasn't far. His jaw tightened. He should have studied the map better. If he had, he would have known that was where they were headed and could have already sent Boggan's men to check it out. Razor probably already had Andi on the boat.

He quickly texted the information to the sheriff and received a message back. The sheriff would send someone to investigate. Then Boggan texted that his men should be reaching Will soon. Will looked at his map again. Boggan was right. His men were to their left and not far away. Then he checked out Indian Creek. It was a pretty good-sized river where a boat could hide anywhere.

He showed Brad the GPS map. "Deputies are here," he said, pointing to a black dot. "If you'll take Chloe to them, I'll go after Andi."

Brad hesitated, and then nodded. "Once she's safe, I'll track you with the deputies' GPS unit."

"I'll leave you a trail to follow."

Will struck out on his own, urgency pushing his body through the undergrowth as he followed the trail of broken branches and disturbed leaves Chloe had left. By the time he reached the rocks Chloe mentioned, every muscle in his legs cried for relief. He scanned the next hill for movement. Nothing. He checked the GPS. If he was reading the map correctly, there were two more ridges between him and the lake.

The whop-whop of a helicopter drew his attention to the air. The massive firefighting copter was headed toward the lake to get water. He text the sheriff to see if they'd spotted Andi and her captors. Nothing. Probably because the bare hardwood trees had switched over to dense pine again.

At least the smoke wasn't nearly as thick now. Pushing on, he descended the hill and climbed the next ridge. Pausing at the top, he sipped the tepid water in the canteen. As he lowered it, movement among the towering pines on the hill across from him caught his eye and he froze. What he wouldn't give for a pair of binoculars right now.

There. He saw it again. Two people, one much smaller. Had to be Andi. Where was the third guy? Yuri, because Razor wouldn't risk leaving Andi with a subordinate. They must have caught sight of him following them.

He found Yuri hiding just above where he planned to cross the creek between the two hills. Nice place for an ambush. *Not this time, buddy.* But first he had to get down the hill he was on without the guy seeing him. He searched for another place to cross and found it a hundred yards above the guy.

Keeping his eye on the man waiting for him, Will worked his way to the creek and wished for the stalking skills of the Cherokee Indians who'd roamed these hills two centuries ago. Once across, he crept around the hill until the man's back was to him.

The man never saw or heard him until Will knocked him out with the butt of his gun. He needed something to tie him with. Will searched the man's jacket and found nothing useful, then spied his boots and jerked the laces out. The man moaned as he dragged him to a small tree. Had to hurry before he came around. Quickly he wrapped his arms around the tree and secured his wrists with the bootlaces.

Then he looked for a handkerchief to gag him and found a bandana in the man's back pocket. By the time he had the gag in place the man was fully awake and trying to get his hands loose.

"You want to go night-night again, Yuri?" Will asked.

His eyes widened and he shook his head.

"Then stop trying to get loose. There's a man right behind me. The woman's brother. I suggest you cooperate since he's not as nice as I am. Understand?"

Yuri nodded.

"Where are they taking the woman?"

He shook his head and said something that sounded like he didn't know.

"Where on Indian Creek is the boat docked?"

The man's eyes widened.

"Yeah, I know about the boat. Where is it?"

Yuri shrugged and shook his head.

"I don't believe you. Tell you what—you have about thirty minutes to think about this before my partner gets here. Maybe a bear won't come along."

The man struggled against the restraint and tried to yell.

"I wouldn't make too much noise. The bears, you know." Then Will turned and jogged up the slope. He figured by the time Brad reached the man he'd be ready to talk. But Will doubted Yuri knew exactly where the boat was docked. He didn't seem the type a boss would confide in.

Will moved stealthily through the trees. He figured Andi was doing her best to slow their pace and he didn't want to alert Razor to his presence. He topped the ridge and his heart sank as water came into sight. Indian Creek.

Revenge

CHAPTER TWENTY-TWO

Razor prodded Andi with his rifle toward the boat at the end of a floating dock. A man who was every bit as tall and muscular as Razor waited on the deck, a rifle in his hands. If she got on the boat, she was dead, or worse. The man shouted something in Latvian and Razor pushed her.

"Get on the boat."

Andi peered at water deep enough to dive into. *Where was Will?* Once they'd started up river, she'd tried to leave him a trail, disturbing the ground or stripping leaves from bushes when she thought Razor wasn't looking.

Razor nudged her with the rifle barrel.

"I'm going," she snapped and hopped onto the dock, rocking it. He jumped right behind her, and the side of the dock tipped up, making him lose his balance. He yelled something in Latvian as Andi dove headfirst into the water. A bullet hit the water, barely nicking her arm. Like a dolphin, she used her feet to propel herself deeper.

***

Will followed the faint trail up the river that Andi had left. He heard her voice then a yell. *They were around the next bend.* Just as he rounded the point, Andi dove into the water and a man on the nearby boat fired at her with a rifle, splatting the water. Another man, had to be Razor, fought to get his balance on a floating dock.

"Police! Drop your weapons!"

The man with the rifle raised it again, and Will fired. The gun dropped, and he fell to the deck as Andi surfaced a few yards from the boat. Razor dove into the water after her.

"Swim to shore!" Will shouted.

She disappeared under the water. Seconds later Razor surfaced with Andi in a chokehold.

No!

"Drop your gun," Razor ordered. He held a knife in his free hand. "If you don't, I'll kill her."

Slowly, Will laid his gun on the ground. "You won't get away."

"But I will. Now back away from the bank."

Will backed to the edge of the woods as Razor pulled Andi toward the finger of land where the water was shallow enough to wade in. Will held his breath as they got their footing. If that knife slipped one inch, it would slice her carotid artery.

Revenge

CHAPTER TWENTY-THREE

Andi's skin burned as the knife pressed against the side of her neck. If Razor stumbled…she pushed the thought away. He moved it slightly as they staggered out of the water, but as soon as they were on firm ground, the blade pressed her skin again.

"If you take one step this way, I'll kill her," Razor yelled.

He meant it, too.

"I'm not moving." Will's hands were balled at his side.

Razor didn't loosen his hold as they walked toward Will's gun on the ground. "If you make the wrong move," he said to Andi, "it will be your last one and his, too. Understand?"

"Yes," she choked out. Death might be better than what he had in mind for her if they got away, but not for Will. *Where was God?*

I'm here. You are mine.

With one arm still securing her, he moved the knife slightly as he bent down to pick up the gun. When his hold loosened, she dug her heels into the ground and shoved, knocking him off balance.

The knife swung upward and nicked her neck before Will crashed into Razor, breaking his hold on her.

They rolled on the ground toward the water.

Andi grabbed Will's gun, but she couldn't get a clear shot.

***

Will grabbed Razor's wrist and squeezed. His fingers

loosened on the knife just as they rolled off the bank and into the water near the boat. Razor pulled him into deeper water. Will kicked to escape the man's grip, but he held fast, and they sank to the bottom.

Will exhaled small amounts of air, buying time. His lungs burned. Razor had to be needing air as bad as Will. He gave one last kick and broke free and shot to the surface, gulping air. Razor surfaced a short distance from him, and Will went after him.

A bullet whizzed past Will's ear, hitting Razor in the chest. Wide-eyed, the man sank as blood colored the water. Will looked over his shoulder, and Andi stood on the bank with his pistol raised, ready to shoot again.

He dove after Razor. The man had disappeared. *What if he got to shore and went after Andi?* Will kicked to the surface and searched for him. When Will saw only Andi, he dove again. *Where was he?* Needing air, he surfaced again, and satisfied Razor was no longer a threat, he swam for the bank. Boggan's men would be here soon. They could find his body.

On shore, Will kept a wary lookout as he wrapped his arms around her shivering body. A trickle of blood ran down her neck. If he'd lost her…he didn't want to go there. "Are you okay?"

She nodded and slipped her arms around his waist and laid her head against his chest. "I thought he was going to drown you. Do you think he's dead, or did he get away?"

"I figure dead, but I don't know. Your shooting was pretty amazing."

She managed a small laugh. "Good thing I wasn't shaking like I am now."

Shouts came from the woods and they turned. Brad and Boggan's deputies.

It truly was over now.

Revenge

CHAPTER TWENTY-FOUR

Andi took the mug of steaming coffee Will held out, her heart thudding at the tenderness in his eyes. She'd barely seen him since yesterday. One of the deputies had brought her back to Living Free and left her with instructions not to leave the building. Will hadn't returned until sometime in the night.

Because Razor hadn't been found, they couldn't walk around the lake or even to the pier. Instead they were sitting in the cafeteria with a dozen other people around. Gingerly, she touched the bandage on her neck. The wound where Razor had cut her with his knife turned out to be superficial as well as where the bullet had grazed her arm. "Any word on Razor?"

"No. They found a couple of jackets on the boat and brought in bloodhounds in case he somehow made it out of the water. The only scent they picked up back-tracked to your trail. And nothing with the cadaver dogs," he said. "There's a team still searching the woods."

"You think he got away?"

"I don't know. I'd like to know what his real name is."

"Maybe one of the men you captured—"

"No. They're not talking. While they're not Russian, I think they belong to the Russian mafia."

That was scary. That particular gang was ruthless and very involved in human trafficking. She shivered, thinking of what might have happened if Will hadn't come after her. "You saved my life."

"I think it was you who saved me. If you hadn't shot Razor..." He studied the cup in his hands. "We need to talk. Alone. Didn't I see a courtyard around here somewhere?"

The seriousness in his voice sent ripples of anxiety through her. Was he going to tell her she was too high maintenance? That he couldn't handle the pressure. Or was it because of the drugs? She hadn't had a chance to tell him she was going to get help with her addiction problem. Not at Living Free because she didn't feel safe here with Razor loose, but somewhere. In fact she was leaving the rehab tomorrow. "I know the area you're talking about."

They left the cafeteria and after winding through the hallways, they came to a small courtyard filled with pots of marigolds and a bench. She bent and snapped off a bloom and held it to her nose. The pungent, musky scent brought back memories of her mother's garden when Andi was a kid. Of being safe. Of a time when she didn't have to face decisions.

Will guided her to the bench in the corner. She rubbed her arms.

"Are you cold?"

"No." Just nervous.

He took his jacket off anyway and put it around her shoulders, and when he sat down beside her, he laced his fingers in hers. Andi studied his hands. Strong. Like he was. She traced a scar with her eyes on his thumb, remembering when he'd gotten it. She'd fallen off her bicycle, trapping her leg, and he'd lifted it off, slicing his knuckle on the fender. Somehow he'd always come to her rescue. What if he didn't want to any longer?

"What do you want to talk about?" she asked, unable to stand the suspense any longer.

At first he didn't answer. "So many things," he said finally. "Yesterday, when I learned you'd been kidnapped, I think I aged twenty years."

She couldn't take any more of this. If he was breaking up

with her, she wanted to get it over with. "Yeah, well I understand if you don't want to be around me any longer."

"What?"

Andi stilled her quivering chin and took a deep breath. "Look, I know I'm always getting in trouble and you always have to save me, and I have this problem with drugs, so I understand if you want to break it off."

"Break it off?" he said. Then he turned to her. "Whoa, wait a minute. Did you say you have problem with drugs?"

She lifted her shoulders in a half shrug. "Yeah. The director is contacting a psychologist for me to see when I get home. I'd stay here, but it might endanger the other patients."

A grin spread across his face. "The important thing is you realize you have a problem."

As much as she'd like to deny it, she couldn't any longer. She stared at the pot of marigolds beside the bench. "That's why I'm so wrong for you. You don't need someone with that kind of problem."

He lifted her chin and turned her face toward him. "It was a problem when you refused to acknowledge it. Now you can get help."

"Really?"

He traced her cheek with his thumb. "I don't know why you think I want to break up with you. When I thought I'd lost you yesterday, the only thing I could think of was finding you and telling you how much I love you."

"Really?" she whispered.

"Yes." He leaned closer and cupped her face in his hands.

His blue eyes held her fast, not that she wanted to get away. She leaned in to him and his lips brushed hers, gently at first, then he pulled her into his arms. Andi slid her arms behind his neck as his lips claimed her again.

When he released her, she sighed. "Does this mean we're still a couple?"

"Depends," he said, slipping his hand into his jacket pocket.

She frowned. "What do you mean?"

Will pulled out a small velvet box. "Andi Hollister, will you marry me?"

Her heart caught in her chest and she forgot to breathe.

"Well?"

"You're not going to get down on one knee?" she teased.

"If that's what it takes."

He moved to get up, and she stopped him. "No, you don't have to do that. Yes, Will Kincade, I will marry you."

Will pulled her into his arms again. "Next week?"

"Tomorrow, if you want."

Revenge

A NOTE TO MY READERS

Dear Reader,

Thank you for reading my novella, *Revenge*. Many of you felt I didn't end Andi Hollister and Will Kincade' story in *Justice Delayed*, the first Memphis Cold Case novel. I didn't want to hurry Andi's addiction recovery, and had thought I would explore it in *Justice Buried*. But as characters sometimes do, they refused to show up, probably wanting more attention than a few paragraphs in *Justice Buried*. But they wouldn't let me alone, so *Revenge* is their story, and aptly named, at that. And don't worry if you haven't read their story in *Justice Delayed*. There aren't any spoilers as far as the suspense and mystery goes.

The following books in the Memphis Cold Case Novels are available or will be available:

- *Justice Delayed* – available now
- *Justice Buried* – available now
- *Justice Betrayed (*available June 2018
- *The fourth book isn't titled, but will deal with human trafficking*

Would you consider signing up for my newsletter? It's a quarterly publication with insider information about the characters in my novels, releases, and whenever my publisher reduces the price on my books, you'll be the first to know. You can sign up here and I'll send you a link to a free novella and short story.

ABOUT PATRICIA BRADLEY

Patricia Bradley lives in North Mississippi with her rescue kitty, Suzy, and is a former abstinence educator and co-author of *RISE To Your Dreams,* an abstinence curriculum. But her heart is tuned to suspense.

Patricia's romantic suspense books include the Logan Point series—*Shadows of the Past, A Promise to Protect, Gone Without a Trace,* and *Silence in the Dark.* Her newest series is the Memphis Cold Case Novels and two have been released—*Justice Delayed* and *Justice Buried.* She has written two sweet romances that are available on Amazon – *Matthew's Choice* and *The Christmas Campaign.*

When she's not spinning tales of suspense and romance, she likes to throw mud on a wheel and see what happens.

Revenge

Books by Patricia Bradley

Memphis Cold Case Novels
Justice Delayed
Justice Buried

Logan Point Series
Shadows of the Past
A Promise To Protect
Gone Without a Trace
Silence In the Dark

Harlequin Heartwarming
Matthew's Choice
The Christmas Campaign

The Gingerbread Pony

Follow Patricia Bradley

Sign up for my no spam newsletter at my website:
www.ptbradley.com

Facebook: https://www.facebook.com/patriciabradleyauthor/

Twitter: https://twitter.com/PTBradley1

BookBub has a new release alert! Not only can you find out the latest deals, you can be the first to know when my next book is available!
Follow me at https://www.bookbub.com/authors/patricia-bradley

Made in the USA
Coppell, TX
02 November 2025

62305230R00056